Totally EUROtic

Communicative classroom activities in
a European context

von Dierk Andresen

Klett Beiträge zum Englischunterricht
in der Erwachsenenbildung

Ernst Klett Verlag für Wissen und Bildung
Stuttgart · Dresden

Totally EUROtic
Communicative classroom activities in a European context

von
Dierk Andresen

unter Leitung und Mitwirkung
der Verlagsredaktion Weiterbildung Englisch
Mitarbeit an diesem Werk:
Margit Duda (Verlagsredakteurin)

Zeichnungen
Annette Karrenbach

Einbandgestaltung
Hanjo Schmidt

For Liz
without whose support this book would never have been written.

Gedruckt auf umweltfreundlichem Recyclingpapier, gefertigt aus 100% Altpapier

1. Auflage 1 4 3 2 1 | 1996 95 94 93

Alle Drucke dieser Auflage können im Unterricht nebeneinander benutzt werden, sie sind untereinander unverändert. Die letzte Zahl bezeichnet das Jahr dieses Druckes.
© Ernst Klett Verlag für Wissen und Bildung GmbH, Stuttgart 1993.
Alle Rechte vorbehalten.
Druck: Süddeutscher Zeitungsverlag, Aalen. Printed in Germany.
ISBN 3-12-537920-2

Contents

Introduction 6

About the activities

Section I: Awareness activities 8
    1. Clarifying national stereotypes 9
    2. The maps in our minds 10
    3. Associations 10
    4. Heaven and hell 11
    5. My Euro shop 12

Section II: Working with pictures and cartoons 13
    1. Picture dictation 14
    2. Picture comparison I 14
    3. Picture comparison II 14
    4. The bonfire 15
    5. Translate your culture 15
    6. Cartoons as a puzzle 16
    7. Look, no words! 16
    8. Pictures of Europe 17
    9. The EC slide lecture 17
    10. My image of the EC 18
    11. Association game 18
    12. Euro stories 19
    13. Get the picture? 20
    14. Where is it? 20
    15. Picture associations 21

Section III: Guessing and problem solving activities 22
    1. Biggest, smallest, flattest 23
    2. The two envelopes 24
    3. What's it all about? 25
    4. Euro charades 26
    5. Find my country 26
    6. Find their country 27

Section IV: Working with foreign language texts ... 28
   1. What language? ... 29
   2. I read the news today ... 29
   3. One out of three ... 30
   4. Translation with a difference ... 30
   5. English – French – English ... 31

Section V: Facts, texts and figures ... 32
   1. Europe by numbers ... 33
   2. The word rose ... 33
   3. Scrambled texts ... 34
   4. Euro diary ... 34
   5. Cutting long stories short ... 35

Section VI: A mixed bag ... 39
   1. Which side are you on? ... 40
   2. Organising pairs: Words don't matter ... 40
   3. Find a European ... 41
   4. Rain in Spain? ... 41
   5. Lucky thirteen ... 42
   6. My Belgium (or Portugal, Greece, etc.) ... 42
   7. If butter mountains were real ... 43
   8. Demonstrations ... 44
   9. Oh, what a night! ... 44
   10. All around Europe ... 44
   11. European treasure chest ... 45
   12. A language learning loop ... 46
   13. Memories of English ... 46
   14. Shopping for Europe ... 47
   15. My Place – the Video ... 48
   16. What if…? ... 48
   17. Euro party ... 49
   18. My European paradise park ... 49
   19. Euro whatsits ... 49
   20. We are the world – We are Europe ... 50
   21. Identity cards ... 51
   22. Don't go to prison! Collect 400 ECUs! ... 52
   23. Choose your own topic ... 52
   24. European love affair ... 53

Useful contact addresses ... 54

Bibliography ... 56

Photocopiable material

Section II: Working with pictures and cartoons 57
   1. Picture dictation 57
   2. Picture comparison I 58
   3. Picture comparison II 60
   4. The bonfire 63
   6. Cartoons as a puzzle 63
   7. Look, no words! 65
  15. Picture associations 67

Section IV: Working with foreign language texts 68
   1. What language? 68
   2. I read the news today 70
   3. One out of three 72
   4. Translation with a difference 73
   5. English – French – English 74

Section V: Facts, texts and figures 77
   1. Europe by numbers 77
   2. The word rose 77
   3. Scrambled texts 79

Section VI: A mixed bag 80
   3. Find a European 80
   4. Rain in Spain? 81
  11. European treasure chest 82
  12. A language learning loop 83
  14. Shopping for Europe 84
  15. My Place – the Video 85
  23. Choose your own topic 86

Make your own EUROtic material

   1. Outline map of the European Community (EC) member states 87
   2. Map of the EC with names of states and capitals 88
   3. Names of all EC states in English 89
   4. Names of all EC states in the national languages 89
   5. Flags of all the EC states 90
   6. The EC member states and their (car) nationality plates 91
   7. EC flag and other cut-out material 93
   8. Map of the EC and neighbouring states 94

Acknowledgements 95

Introduction

Why this book?

Europe is growing together. Twelve European states are committed to the development of closer economic and political cooperation. Others are waiting to join them.

The European Community has agreed to break down the economic and political barriers that have existed for so long. Greater free movement of goods, services, capital and people between the EC's member states is the main objective.

Trade barriers can be lifted within a very short time. Once they have been abolished through the usual legal processes they no longer exist. Other barriers may take longer to break down.

In a Europe that is growing together, language barriers are one of the most difficult obstacles to overcome. And although many Europeans – at least the better-off ones – have travelled widely across the continent, the knowledge of the culture, of the political systems and of everyday life in the neighbouring states is generally very limited.

In the foreign language classroom this new Europe is not yet much of a topic. But with the proposed changes coming into force and increasingly affecting the lives of millions of people, this new reality will be a topic of conversation. Only very few language course books currently available deal with this topic; and that is where this book comes in.

A new approach to Europe

EC policies do not please all the people all of the time, to say the least. In fact, some of these policies can turn one off Europe. This book is meant to turn you on to the idea of a European Community of people (not of bureaucracies, multinational companies or governments). Its aim is not to give unequivocal support to everything that comes from *Brussels*. This book has been written to help people – within Europe and outside of it – talk about the changes that are and will be taking place. Only through a good command of foreign languages will the millions of people in Europe who do not have access to interpreters become a European nation.

The activities in this book also attempt to stimulate interest in what is going on outside the language learners' home countries. Trying to learn one's neighbours' languages, and trying to understand their culture, is an important prerequisite for a harmonious relationship.

Totally EUROtic is not a socio-political textbook. It aims towards a better understanding of life in Europe by making students' experiences come alive in the classroom and providing a framework for discussion of European topics.

This does not mean that the teacher will have to take a course in European affairs before tackling this subject in class. On the contrary, most of the exercises provided do **not** require any prior detailed knowledge of the EC.

This book is a collection of communicative activities and games which bring Europe to life in the classroom. The range of exercises provided reflects, at least to some extent, the development in teaching techniques over the last few years. It is the student that is the centre of attention, and not a textbook which has to be worked through. This collection of activities also tries to show that almost any topic can be turned into a starting point for stimulating classroom work. There are, of course, many more Euro activities that could be done in the classroom than have found their way into this book. To help teachers create their own material this book not only provides a lot of ready-to-use photocopiable material for the classroom in the form of worksheets or texts. Maps, flags and other material reproducible in black and white are provided as well, so that teachers can make their own worksheets look more European without having to go hunting for suitable originals.

For some exercises current material (*political cartoons, newspaper texts,* etc.) is required. This the book could not provide, as it would date too quickly. There are enough suggestions in the book, however, to give teachers an idea of what they should look for.

Although this book has been written in English and with the teacher of English as a foreign language in mind, almost all the games are suitable for courses in other foreign languages and usually do not require any further preparation.

In fact, quite a few of the activities encourage the students to lose their fear of other languages and even to try and gather information from languages that they are not familiar with.

To those readers who have been using games in the classroom for some time, several activities will look familiar. I have, in fact, adapted some classic games to the European context. To other readers this book might serve as an introduction to more communicative ways of teaching foreign languages.

Another group of people might also find this book useful: people who organize international meetings of young people or functions at the town twinning level.

All these games have been successfully tested in the classroom, both in regular courses dealing with Europe and in seminars and weekend courses.

Wherever the reader opens the book, each section provides instantly usable ideas for the teacher. Some need extra preparation, made much easier, however, by the wide collection of copiable material in the second part of the book.

To sum up the intentions I had in writing this book: I wanted to show that Europe need not be a dry and dusty topic. It can and should be fun – especially in the classroom.

Author's note: Summer 1992

When I set out to collect ideas for making Europe a topic of my English courses, media attention was very much focused on the EC. This is reflected in many of the activities presented here. In the first years of this decade, however, Europe has changed considerably – too much, in fact, to be taken into account in this collection. But rather than try and adapt the games to a rapidly changing situation, I have stuck to the original concept of concentrating on the EC. The activities, can, however, be equally suitably applied to dealing with other European countries.

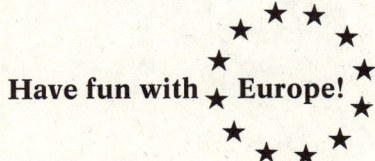

Section I
Awareness activities

Although the European Community has often been in the news, few hard facts about the EC have reached the general public. It is therefore better not to take any knowledge for granted.

Your students are likely, however, to have travelled in several EC countries, been to Italian and Greek restaurants, and even visited Paris, London or Rome. They will also have heard at least something about the EC through the media and will thus have some images of Europe in their minds. These could range from songtitles such as *Tulips from Amsterdam* and stereotypical associations *(Italy/Mafia)* to factual or erroneous bits of political know-how (e.g. *Britain is the dirty man of Europe. The British are dragging their feet when it comes to putting EC regulations into national law.*)

The exercises in this first section are designed to draw out what the students already know, to help them acquire and practise useful vocabulary, in particular the names of the EC countries, their people, their languages and much more related vocabulary.

I. Awareness activities

1. Clarifying national stereotypes

This exercise helps to focus students' attention on national stereotypes. This sort of activity works particularly well in mixed-nationality classes but can also be successfully used with culturally homogeneous groups.
Language level required: upper intermediate. The exercise takes about fifteen to thirty minutes.

Procedure Discuss with your class how a diagram such as the one below could make sense, e.g. in what way could the given nationalities be seen as *opposites*.

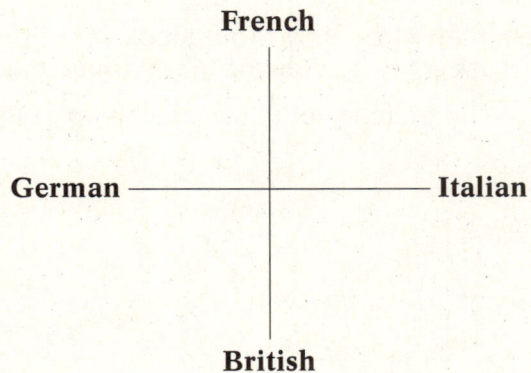

Then ask the students where they would put the other EC nationalities.

I. Awareness activities

2. The maps in our minds

When asked to draw maps of their own countries people usually overstate the size of their immediate neighbourhood or region and let the rest of the country shrink to a rather non-descript appendix of the better-known bit. In making students aware of this they will realize how distorted their mental map of Europe is. This exercise takes about five to fifteen minutes and can be done with post-beginners. It was suggested to me by *Mario Rinvolucri*.

Procedure Ask students to draw a map of the EC countries to the best of their ability. Tell them that this is not a geography test but that it will eventually serve to give them a clearer picture of Europe's geography.

Once the students have drawn their maps they should look at the results of their fellow students' work and discuss errors and distortions with them in pairs.

Only after this phase has been completed should a correct map of Europe or the EC countries be presented.

3. Associations

This game gets students to talk about their memories of and associations with the various EC countries. The game should not focus on general knowledge but on the ideas that students associate with the EC countries. They might associate California with sunshine and sunshine with Spain, so they would perhaps put No. 1 on the Mediterranean Spanish coast. On the other hand they might associate California with surfing and remember their own attempts at surfing during a holiday on the North Sea. There are, of course, no *correct* solutions.

I. Awareness activities

The object of the game is to make students aware of their views on Europe. The result is often a mixture of associations based on facts (this happens for example when students associate *Hollywood* with the centre of the European film industry) or a very personal experience.

Various lists could be used (see example below). When I started working with this game, I used the following list of *Americana* but many other words would serve the purpose of the game equally well.

The game takes about fifteen to thirty minutes and can be done from an intermediate level upwards.

Preparation Bring copies of a map of the EC countries to class. You will need one per student. The map need not show more than the outlines of the various countries.

Procedure Hand out the maps to the students.

Dictate a set of about fifteen numbered words. The words provided should not have any easily detectable objective connotations with the various countries as this would turn the game into a general knowledge quiz.

Let students write down the words and put the *numbers* onto their maps according to their own associations.

Once all fifteen numbers and words have been dictated ask students to discuss their associations in pairs or groups of three to four.

If students seem to dry up, get the class together again in one group and ask for some of the associations that others had. Also try to find out which countries were left out – a useful piece of information that shows the *blind spots* on people's mental maps.

Euro America

1. California
2. John F. Kennedy
3. Chinatown
4. Hollywood
5. NASA
6. New York City
7. Texas
8. Drugs
9. Alaska
10. Washington DC
11. Abraham Lincoln
12. Los Angeles
13. McDonalds
14. Disneyland
15. CIA

4. Heaven and hell

In this exercise students will be confronted with (strong) stereotypical views of various European nationalities. The exercise takes about ten to fifteen minutes and can be done with lower intermediate students.

Procedure Hand out the following instructions and text to students:

Someone once made a statement about Europe that read something like this:

"Heaven is where the police are _____, the cooks _____,

the mechanics _____, the lovers _____ and it is all organised by

the _____.

I. Awareness activities

Hell is where the cooks are _____, the mechanics _____, the lovers _____, the police _____, and it is all organised by the _____."

You realize, of course, that the nationalities have been left out in the above text.

Here are some suggestions for the missing nationalities. Not all of them will appear in the text:

British / Swiss / Spanish / Italians / Dutch / Germans / Belgians / Irish / Portuguese / Russians / Swedes / Danes / Luxembourgers / Austrians / Poles / French / etc.

Discuss the choices with your fellow students. How do you think the original text was worded? Would you have written the text differently? Give reasons for your choices.

The original text, whose origin is obscure, ran like this:

> Heaven is where the police are *British*, the cooks *Spanish*, the mechanics *German*, the lovers *Italian* and it is all organised by the *Swiss*.
> Hell is where the cooks are *British*, the mechanics *Spanish*, the lovers *Swiss*, the police *German*, and it is all organised by the *Italians*.

5. My Euro shop

Most people are quite used to being able to buy goods from other countries in the shops. Some, of course, are harder to come by than others. And for many items one has to go to the big cities or even to the countries of origin to buy them. This game uses the individual preferences of the learners as its background. On a simple level it can be played by post-beginners. It might be more rewarding, however, for intermediate students. The game takes about ten to twenty minutes.

Procedure Explain the situation described above. Then ask the students to write down what they personally would like to find in a *Euro shop* near the place where they live; such a shop would provide them with all the goods they would otherwise have to travel some distance to buy. Students then share their lists in pairs or small groups.

Section II
Working with pictures and cartoons

Pictures and cartoons can be a very stimulating medium in the classroom and they are not hard to come by, even if you are looking for material dealing with aspects of life in the European Community. Within Europe many illustrated magazines carry articles on the various member countries. Travel brochures can also be a good source especially for pictures of tourist spots. The press and information offices of the various embassies issue excellent material and it is often given away free. Then there are, of course, the various EC institutions which publish quite a wide selection of brochures and magazines. If you do not have easy access to magazines ask students to help you out with their discarded ones. They will often be only be too willing to help. As for political cartoons, you can find them in British newspapers or your national ones; they do not necessarily have to be in the target language.

The exercises in this section make use of pictures and cartoons for various purposes: to enlarge vocabulary, for guessing games and for other games in which students can play with their imagination. Photos, paintings, drawings and cartoons can all be excellent material. Once you start looking around, you will find useful pictures in the most unlikely sources.

II. Working with pictures and cartoons

1. Picture dictation

This game is another classic information gap activity in which students get instant feedback on how well they have expressed themselves. It can be played at a lower intermediate level and often earlier. One round takes about ten to fifteen minutes.
This game is based on an idea by *Mario Rinvolucri*.

Preparation Collect graphics that have an EC theme. Cut them out and stick them onto paper or cardboard. It is usually advisable to put the prepared pictures in a folder so that students will later have something in which to hide their pictures from their partners. Sample cartoons are provided on page 57 but magazines often provide colourful material. Students should bring pencils and erasers to class.

Procedure Pair off students and give one member of each pair a picture. Tell them to make sure their partner cannot see it.

The student with the picture then describes it to his/her partner giving him/her as much information as necessary to be able to make a fair copy of the original if only in outline. The other student listens to the explanations and tries to draw the picture accordingly. He/she is allowed to ask questions. In fact both partners in this game are encouraged to exchange as much information as possible, short of showing the picture itself to the student trying to draw it before he/she has finished.

2. Picture comparison I

Picture comparison is a well-known form of communication gap exercise. This variation requires picture sets with EC contents. Teachers who do not see themselves as skillful enough draughtsmen can cut out elements from political or other cartoons that show European politicians, scenes and events. These can then be combined to make a picture. By rearranging the various elements, adding or altering some bits, a second version containing eight to ten differences can be made without difficulty. The exercise requires pair work, can be done from a lower intermediate level onwards and takes about ten minutes. A copiable set of pictures can be found on pages 58 and 59.

Preparation Construct two pictures differing in the way described above. Make enough copies of these so that you will be able to provide each pair of students with one pair of (not identical) pictures.

Procedure Students sit in pairs opposite each other. They are given the pictures and exchange information about them in order to find the differences between the two pictures. The exercise is finished when they have found all the differences.

3. Picture comparison II

This game is another version of *Picture comparison I*. If the Euro-elements you have collected from political cartoons and brochures cannot be composed into a coherent picture they can still be of use for a communicative exercise. This exercise also takes about ten minutes and is suitable for lower intermediate students upwards.

II. Working with pictures and cartoons

Preparation   Collect a number of political cartoons that deal with the EC as well as graphics from EC brochures. Cut out some of the elements of those pictures and stick them into a copy of the twelve empty frames provided on page 62. Make another copy of the empty frames and fill them with slightly altered versions (things left out, added, changed, order of pictures changed) of the original twelve pictures.

If you cannot find enough material, copy the two sets of pictures on pages 60 and 61.

Make as many copies of each set as necessary to provide half the class with one sheet.

Procedure   Students sit in pairs opposite each other describing their picture. They have to find as many differences between the two pictures as possible.

4. The bonfire

This game is just one example of how cartoons can be used as a lead-in into a discussion of EC policies, in this case environmental policy. The resulting discussion could focus on the question how EC regulations will affect the lives of ordinary citizens and what their reactions towards such regulations could be. The fact that this cartoon relates to EC affairs should not be mentioned so as not to spoil the surprise element. The guessing part (five to ten minutes) can be done from a lower intermediate level upwards. A discussion requires a higher standard of fluency.

Preparation   Prepare an OHP transparency of the cartoon on page 63 with the words in the speech bubble missing.

Procedure   Project the cartoon and ask the class to describe what the man is doing. Ask them what they think the woman is saying. (It is, of course, unlikely that they will think of the EC in these situations unless that subject has already been introduced.)

When they have put forward several suggestions, ask them for the most likely one.

Uncover the text.

Ask the class what is funny about the cartoon, what sort of image of the EC is presented in this cartoon, whether they have ever felt personally affected by an EC ruling.

This could then be used as a lead-in into a discussion of environmental issues, a discussion of a topical text on EC environmental policy, or a discussion about whether the EC should have powers to regulate environmental affairs.

5. Translate your culture

It is often difficult to understand political cartoons from another country because one does not know the country or the leading political figures. Explanations are necessary. This game takes about fifteen minutes and is best played from an intermediate level upwards.

II. Working with pictures and cartoons

Preparation Collect a number of political cartoons involving an EC theme and politicians from your country or a point of discussion topical in your country.

Procedure Students sit in pairs and are given a political cartoon. One of them has to pretend to be from another EC country and not able to make sense of the political cartoon in front of them. The task of the other student is to explain the cartoon in detail. The *foreign* student should ask as many questions as possible.

6. Cartoons as a puzzle

This game can be used as a lead-in into a discussion on a political topic or just as a quick, plain, guessing game. It can be played at lower intermediate level or earlier and takes about five to ten minutes. A sample cartoon can be found on pages 63 and 64. It was used as a lead-in into a text on air-traffic chaos in Britain, see page 64.

Preparation Take a political cartoon, preferably one with a caption rather than speech bubbles and copy it onto an OHP transparency. It should contain a lot of detail. Put a non-transparent sheet of paper over this copy and cut little *windows* into it with a paper knife so that some important and some misleading items can be seen.

Procedure Put the transparency onto the OHP (switched off at this stage). Cover the *windows* with bits of paper.

Switch on the OHP and uncover one *window*. Let the students guess what the rest of the picture will be about.

Uncover the second *window* and ask for more guesses and so on until the last *window* has been opened. There will be a process of constant reappraisal in the students' guessing, with the last *window* being opened as a sort of punchline or a final clue from which the students could guess at the topic of the cartoon or its caption.

7. Look, no words!

Rather than giving students an introductory lecture on the various policy fields the EC is engaged in, you could ask them to speculate or make informed guesses on those fields. They can use all the background knowledge they might have. To be played from an intermediate level upwards, the game takes about ten to twenty minutes depending on how much detail you want to go into.

Preparation Cut five to eight photos out of EC brochures describing EC policy. Many of the photos will be ambiguous, deriving their meaning from the context in which they are found. Prepare them in such a way that the class can see them (wall poster, OHP transparency or photocopy). A copiable set of pictures can be found on pages 65 and 66.

Very useful EC brochures for this purpose are *Consumer Policy in the Single Market, Environmental Policy in the European Community* and *Energy in the European Community*.

II. Working with pictures and cartoons

Procedure   Students form two or more groups depending on the size of the class. With the help of the pictures they have to define what policy fields the EC is engaged in. In a small class you can work directly with the whole group. If you have more than one group let them discuss the pictures among themselves first and then have a whole-group session later. They should write down their findings in simple sentences.

8. Pictures of Europe

This exercise focuses mainly on vocabulary. It can be done at a fairly elementary level but more advanced students will also find it challenging. This exercise can take up a good half hour but can also be done at a quicker pace.
Beware: Students are sometimes quite puzzled by the fact that the English names for places and famous sights are different from those in their mother-tongue and tend to *anglicize* the terms they know from their mother-tongue. Do not worry that students will find the cutting-out part too childish. They usually love it.

Preparation   Bring to class (or ask your students to bring) a pile of travel brochures and all sorts of magazines. Make sure scissors, sheets of blank paper and glue are available.

Procedure   Hand out the magazines. Students should have access to as much material as possible.

Students cut out pictures of European things/people/places from the magazines and stick them onto their sheets of paper.

They then name the things on their sheets and/or write short texts about them. They should however, make sure they have got the correct English words. They could check with a dictionary or with you.

Next they show their collage to a fellow student and explain it.

In a second round, they could present it to the whole class (if the class is not too big).

9. The EC slide lecture

This exercise is best used after the students have done some work on the EC. It will be more fun to them as well as more challenging to incorporate newly learned facts into the lecture they will have to give. The preparation should take about fifteen minutes, the presentation another fifteen minutes depending on the group. This game works best from an upper intermediate level onwards.

Preparation   Bring about fifteen slides to class. The slides should not have anything to do with the EC. You can use any slides you might have at home, even blurred ones. Perhaps you could especially prepare some confusing ones with close-ups of single everyday objects. Slides obviously taken outside EC countries can also be very intriguing. If need be, you could take pictures or photos out of magazines.

II. Working with pictures and cartoons

Procedure Take some of your students to another room. Tell them that they are in the following situation:

> "You are visiting a friend who lives in a small town in South America. She knows that you speak English very well. There is an English Club in the town and your friend is the president of it. In a letter she asked you whether you could give a lecture on *Everyday life in the EC today.* You willingly agreed. You went through all your slides choosing some taken at home and some during your holidays in various EC countries. You also sorted out some slides to throw away, for one reason or another.
> Now is the great day. The room in which you are to give the lecture is already filled with people. Everybody is excited because they all love slide lectures. Your talk is to start in about half an hour after some other club matters have been dealt with. Just to make sure, you go through your box of slides again, only to find that you have packed the wrong slides – the ones you wanted to throw away. You have no choice. The people out there want to see slides! There is no way you can give your talk without slides. You just have to rearrange your talk around the slides you have with you. Lying to the audience about what the slides show could perhaps be risky as some of them have been to Europe…"

Give the group about fifteen minutes to prepare their lecture. Occupy the rest of the class with a completely different activity or discuss with them what they would expect to see in a slide lecture with the title *Everyday life in the EC today*. Then call the other group back and let them present their lecture. Make sure they are talking **to** the audience rather than to you or the slides!

10. My image of the EC

This exercise gives students a chance to clarify their own view of the EC and share their views with their fellow students. It can be done from an intermediate level onwards and takes about ten to twenty minutes. In large classes, groups of five to seven students should be formed.

Preparation Collect a set of large (at least A5) pictures from magazines. They should not have anything to do with the EC. You should have about thirty to fifty per cent more pictures than you have students in your class.

Procedure Put the pictures on a table. Ask students to go to the table and, without talking, choose a picture that reminds them of the EC in some way.
They then go back to their seats with their picture and tell the class or their group what made them choose it.

11. Association game

This game combines story telling from pictures with, possibly, political and other factual information on the EC. It is best played at an intermediate level or above and takes about twenty minutes.

II. Working with pictures and cartoons

Preparation Cut out pictures referring to EC countries (national costumes, monuments, language items, cartoons, maps, etc.). You should have at least five pictures per student.

Mount the pictures on cards. For easier storage the cards should be of the same size. They might come in handy for other games later. For greater durability you could also laminate them.

Mix these pictures with others that only indirectly refer to the EC and some that have nothing to do with the EC at all.

Bring these pictures to class.

Procedure Students sit in groups of four to six around a table. Each student gets five to seven pictures.

One picture is put in the middle of the table.

Students roll a die to find out who is going to start.

The first student then puts one of his pictures next to the picture that is already on the table. That student then has to find a *link* between the first picture and the one he has put next to it. The group then decides by majority decision whether the link made is valid. This should not be taken too seriously. If they accept the link, the turn passes on to the next student. If a student cannot find a link between any one of his pictures and the one that has been put down last, the turn passes to the next student. The winner is the first student who has placed all his pictures.

Students are not allowed to place more than one picture at a time.

12. Euro stories

This exercise asks students to make up stories using pictures as cues. It is a speaking and listening exercise similar to *Chinese whispers,* where an original statement gets distorted as it is passed on from student to student. The game works well at all levels above lower intermediate. The time required depends on the number of groups that are formed and hence on the number of times the stories are retold. As a variation you could add a bit of text, e.g. a very short newspaper article or just a headline or a well-known date instead of one of the pictures.

Preparation Collect twice as many pictures as there are students in your class. A quarter of these pictures should have a clear link to an EC country.

Procedure Students organise themselves into groups of four.

Each group gets six to eight pictures. Two of the pictures should have some obvious relation to an EC country (famous landmark/politician/street scene/part of a map/, etc.). The other pictures should be chosen at random.

Students then make up a story incorporating all their six to eight pictures.

When all groups have done this, two students from each group move on to the next group clockwise.

The two students who remain with their pictures tell their story to the *newcomers.*

II. Working with pictures and cartoons

These in turn stay as another exchange takes place. The students who have just heard the story tell it to the new pair of students.

The process is repeated until the original group has formed again. They can then tell each other how their original story got distorted in the process.

13. Get the picture?

This is a very lively game involving two teams of players. It can be played from post-beginner level and serves to revise vocabulary. Depending on the number of pictures, it takes about ten to fifteen minutes.

Preparation Collect a large number of pictures of at least A5 size and stick them onto cardboard. Find one or two words or a phrase for each picture so that they could be easily identified by somebody flicking through them. Here are some ways in which words and pictures can be linked:

Example:

Words	Picture
Fast and French	– Concorde
British and blue	– Tory MP
To be or not to be	– Danish castle or British actor
Rain on the plain	– Spanish landscape
Agricultural policy	– Apples being destroyed

Procedure The class is put into two teams both of which should stand behind one or more tables. Each team has in front of it half the number of pictures spread out so that they can be seen.

The teacher then calls a word or phrase and the teams have to find amongst their pictures one that matches the phrase. The team which finds a suitable picture first keeps it. The first team to collect ten pictures wins the game.

14. Where is it?

For this exercise you need pictures that show a scene which is not immediately identifiably British or French or Belgian but which contains clues that make the careful observer 90% certain that his/her identification of the country is correct. The language level is lower intermediate and the exercise takes about ten minutes.

Preparation Collect a set of pictures as described above. You will not need many: five to ten will be enough. They should however, be big enough to be identified by students standing around a table.

II. Working with pictures and cartoons

Procedure Put the pictures on a table or on the floor and ask students to stand around them. (If you have a large class, you could do the exercise in two groups with different pictures.) Then ask students to identify the various countries shown in the pictures without any help from you. Give them a time limit to give you their verdict. To make sure they cooperate more closely get one of the students to note down their conclusions which must be majority decisions. If you have two groups you can let them compete: who gets the most pictures right?

15. Picture associations

The exciting thing about the following game is that it shows once more how differently students react to the same input. The game can be played from a lower intermediate level upwards depending on the difficulty of the text you choose. It takes about fifteen to thirty minutes.

Most kinds of texts can be used for this game: straightforward bits of EC news, human interest stories, literary excerpts, etc. There should however, be some European context.
Two sample texts are provided on page 67.

Preparation Choose a text you want to work with. It should be very close to the students' level so that they can understand it in one reading.

Bring a set of about fifty pictures taken out of magazines, etc. to class. Some of them should be complete scenes, others just details of things. (Such a picture set can be used for many different exercises, so it might be worth sticking them onto stiff paper.)

Procedure Read out the text to the class.

Spread all pictures on a desk and ask each student to choose a picture that he or she can somehow associate with the text.

They should then sit down and either discuss their choice with one or more partners, or, if the class is small enough, present their picture and their association to the whole group.

Section III

Guessing and problem solving activities

Guessing games in all their variety are a favourite activity with students of all ages. Whereas many such activities let the class play against a knowledgeable teacher, the games presented here are often more communicative, i.e. letting students play against each other. The games and activities in this section do not generally require much knowledge of EC affairs. Of course, these games can be played at a more sophisticated level with groups who are more deeply involved with EC topics.

III. Guessing and problem solving activities

1. Biggest, smallest, flattest

This guessing game also gives the students a fair amount of input on the various EC countries.
One round can take only a few minutes to play, but if students keep losing points it could go on for twenty to thirty minutes. The game can be played from a lower intermediate level upwards.

Preparation Before class collect a fair number of facts on each EC country. If you are planning to work more extensively on the EC, start a file in which you collect such data combining general knowledge with surprising facts. Depending on the skill of the students you might need more sets of facts than just for five countries.

Procedure Divide the class into two teams. Tell students that they will have to find out the name of an EC country.

The winner is the first group to collect five points.

Read out one-sentence statements about the country of your choice. As soon as a group thinks they have the answer, they can shout *Capital* and name it as proof of the correct guess. If they get the country right, they win one point. If they get it wrong, they lose three points; this is to discourage indiscriminate guessing. Groups should, of course, confer.

Teams who guess the name should give reasons for their choice.

Example:

- When you were a child someone might have read you fairy tales by an author from this country. (H. C. Andersen)
- There is a daily ferry service between this country and Britain.
- Its neighbour to the north is a monarchy. (Sweden)
- The biggest part of it is not in the EC. (Greenland)
- Its highest mountain is 173 meters high.
  The country is, of course, Denmark.

Here are some more examples of facts you could use for your sentences:

Portugal is hardly bigger than Austria.
Portugal is the poorest country in Western Europe.
Portugal used to be a world power.
The Netherlands is the most densely populated country in Europe.
The Netherlands is the only EC country – next to Britain – that has almost as much energy as it needs. (gas)
Half the Dutch population are Catholics.
Luxembourg is the smallest state of the EC.
Luxembourg has the highest ratio of foreigners in the EC. (26%)
Ireland is about as big as Bavaria.
The world's most beautiful golf courses are said to be in Ireland.
Britain used to be the most important power in the world.
Denmark is the flattest country in the EC.
Greenland is 50 times as big as Denmark.
France is the biggest state in the EC.
Belgium generates 50 percent of its wealth through exports.

III. Guessing and problem solving activities

2. The two envelopes

Learning to co-operate is essential for students who are involved in a language course that engages them actively in a lot of activities. The idea for the following exercise owes a lot to the *Word-Letter* exercise suggested in *A Handbook of Structured Experiences For Human Relations Training* (Pfeiffer, J. W. / Jones, J. E., San Diego, California 1977). This activity is for intermediate students and takes about twenty to thirty minutes.

Preparation Prepare a large manila envelope that contains two more envelopes, each with twenty to twenty-five EC-related words. These should be written on cards with a marker pen so that they are easily readable. They should also contain instruction sheets (see below).

Procedure Split the class into two groups. One group – the inner group, seated around a table or in a circle on the floor will be solving a task, while the other one – the outer group, standing or sitting around the first group will act as observers. Ask one of the groups to be the inner group. The inner group takes the manila envelope, opens it, removes one of the smaller envelopes in which they will find an instruction sheet stating:

> This envelope contains cards on which words have been written. Your task is to arrange these cards.

It will then be up to the group to decide *how* to arrange the cards. There is no single *correct* solution.

The task of the outer group is to observe how the inner group goes about solving the task and perhaps take notes on how individual group members contributed to or hindered the solving of the problem.

The first envelope should contain words in various languages rather than just in the target language. Some of the words should be ambiguous, i.e. should possibly belong to more than one language.

Example:

> French / Obrigado / Britisher / Rome / Rom / Londres / Italy / Milano / Milan / Milanese / Dane / Frankreich / Merci / Inglese / Anglais / Hollanda / Denmark / Royaume-Unie / Dansk / Portugal / Zero / English / Briton / Holland / Si / No / Gaelic / Brittany / Germania / Hello / Luxembourg / etc.

When the group has decided it has completed the task, hold a feedback session in which the outer group comments on its observations. The process is then reversed, i.e. the groups change position. The new inner group takes out the second envelope, which contains the same instructions.

The second envelope could contain words from one of the EC languages not (well) known to the group. To decide on this, one needs to have at least a vague idea of the students' knowledge of languages. One could, of course, go for a language most certainly not known well by the students e.g. Welsh or Gaelic. Words can be randomly selected from a suitable dictionary.

III. Guessing and problem solving activities

Example: (Dutch words)

> zelden / spoedig / kweken / pannekoek / beurs / wedstrijd / somber / leraar / orgeldraaier / postzegel / oom / tuin / jammer / krantenkiosk / week / trein / politie / stoep / nieuwsgierig / zak / leuk / stipt

For interest's sake you could provide a translation of the words afterwards. This, obviously, would have no bearing on the *solution*.

3. What's it all about?

This game allows students a lot of spontaneity and can be great fun. It is best played from an intermediate level onwards. The game takes about twenty to thirty minutes (plus fifteen minutes preparation time for three of the students).

Preparation Copy the following text onto a sheet of paper and bring it to class.

Procedure Take three students out of the classroom and give them the following text.

> "It's Brussels, isn't it?"
> Alec didn't answer.
> "It's another one of these committees, isn't it?"
> Susan started to cry.
> Alec wanted to console her but couldn't bring himself do so. He hated having had to tell her now. She had been so proud this morning and rightly so. And now this.
> "It's always your life, isn't it? Never mine."
> "That's not fair."
> He heard a key turn in the front door. It was Pierre who glanced quickly in their direction as he passed. He nodded to Alec, ignoring Susan and went straight up to his room. Should he tell him Alec wondered but then decided against it. What business was it of his?
> Silence. At last Susan said, "Have you told Carmen?"
> Carmen! He had completely forgotten about her.

They have to make sense of it and find a context for this scene, i.e. discuss and agree on who the people are, what has just happened, who the other people mentioned in the text are, etc.

After fifteen minutes – or earlier if they are ready – ask the three students to come back and present the text partly as a role-play *(Susan and Alec)* and partly by reading aloud to the other students who sit in a half circle in front of the actors.

Once the scene has been presented the other students have to ask *Yes/No* questions to find out what the background to the dialogue is.

The teacher then tries to get all the other students involved by spontaneously assigning them roles in the following manner:

III. Guessing and problem solving activities

Example:

> "Melanie, you are Susan's best friend, what will she do now?"
> "George, you are Alec's boss. Are you happy with his work?"
> "Ingrid, you are Alec's secretary. How did he react when George told him of the decision."
> "Julian, you were Susan's first husband. Why did you get divorced?"

The exercise has to be done very quickly. Do not hesitate to move on to another person if a student cannot cope with his role and cannot find anything interesting to say.

4. Euro charades

This game will work better if students have already done a bit of work on Europe but usually there is enough background knowledge around to make it work without any preparation. The game can occasionally be over in less than a minute, in which case just play another round. It can be played from lower intermediate upwards.

Procedure Ask a volunteer to come to the front of the class. Give her or him a card with the name of an EC country or nationality written on it.

The student should then mime that country or nationality. The other students have to guess it.

As soon as a student thinks he or she has found the country they should shout *Stop!*, name the country and give reasons for their decision.

The student performing then stops, or goes on if the guess has been a wrong one.

Variation Instead of one country the student mimes three in a row and the other students have to guess afterwards which countries they were.

5. Find my country

This game requires close cooperation and group decision-making. It is best played only by students who already have some knowledge of EC countries, as they are very likely to lose if they just take pot shots at one country after another.

The game takes about fifteen minutes and can be done from an intermediate level upwards.

Procedure Put the students into two groups.

Think of an EC country and tell students

- that they have to guess it
- that you are only going to anwer *Yes/No* questions
- that they are not allowed to ask more than five questions (or put the limit at three with more advanced groups).

III. Guessing and problem solving activities

The students should discuss possible questions among themselves before asking them.

They take turns asking questions.

Example:

> S: "Is it a Mediterranean country?"
> T: "No." (out go Spain, France, Italy and Greece)
> S: "Does it border the Baltic?"
> T: "No." (out go Germany and Denmark)
> S: "Is it one of the original six EC countries?"
> T: "Yes." (out go Great Britain, Ireland and Portugal)
> S: "Can you go there by ferry from Britain?"
> T: "No." (out go Belgium and the Netherlands)
> S: "Then it must be Luxembourg."
> T: "You're right. It is Luxembourg."

The winner is the group that gets the answer most quickly or with the least number of questions.

6. Find their country

This game can be prepared either as homework or in class. It might give the students more scope if they already have some information on the EC. The preparation takes about ten to fifteen minutes. The game itself can be over in a few minutes, in which case one would go on to another pair of students. It can be played from an upper intermediate level upwards. Instead of countries, one can of course, agree to talk about another EC-related topic.

Preparation   Either in class or as homework, get pairs of students to prepare a dialogue which they will later present to the class. The dialogue should be about an EC country without giving away the identity of the country too easily.

Procedure   Get a pair of students to read out or perform their dialogue in front of the class. The task of the other students is to guess the name of the country. Students who think they have got it should write the name of the country on a slip of paper and pass it to the performing pair. If they are right they are allowed to join the conversation – again trying not to give away the country too easily.

Section IV

Working with foreign language texts

It might seem strange to be working with texts in, say, Dutch or Italian when the aim of the class is to learn English, and initially you may encounter some student resistance to the idea. Being able to understand and extract information from a range of foreign language texts, even on a passive level only, will however be an increasingly useful skill.

The usual student attitude will probably be *I don't know French/Dutch/Danish*, etc.

The following exercises try to break down negative attitudes to this sort of work and gently demonstrate that students can indeed cope with texts that seem at first sight to be absolutely foreign.

Suitable texts can be acquired from the EC institutions, who publish most texts in all nine official EC languages. For other material, international newsagents at big railway stations usually have a wide selection of newspapers and magazines.

IV. Working with foreign language texts

1. What language?

Talking about and working with foreign language texts will eventually make the other languages feel less threatening. It also practises the important nationality words.

The following exercise requires group cooperation and can be done from post-beginners level. Depending on how many texts you hand out, the exercise takes about ten minutes.

Preparation Prepare copies of assorted foreign language texts to make it more lively. Take a mix of short excerpts, including cartoons and advertisements. There should be about five to seven texts reproduced on one worksheet (copiable samples can be found on pages 68 and 69). Number the individual texts.

Procedure Students sit in groups of four to five and are given copies of the worksheets.

Their task is

a) to determine the languages in which the texts on the worksheets are written

b) to sort them into official EC languages and non-EC languages.
Students should try not to take wild guesses but as far as possible find proof for their decisions.

When they have finished they should report their findings to the whole class.

2. I read the news today

Target language only teachers should not be put off this exercise, which gives practice in the vital skill of paraphrasing.

The texts used in this exercise are mother-tongue newspaper articles (or passages out of books) dealing with the EC or events in EC countries. The texts should be well above the language level of the students so that they would surely fail if they tried to translate them. Texts of twenty to forty lines are most suitable. In choosing the texts you should look at the relevance of the information provided. The content of the news items might come in useful in later discussions. Some sample texts in German are provided on pages 70 and 71.

This exercise works best at an upper intermediate level. Students may find it very demanding at first but will find they enjoy the challenge as they go on. The exercise takes about fifteen to thirty minutes. Each student should be given the chance to paraphrase at least one text.

Preparation Bring to class a selection of short newspaper articles. One per student is ideal. You should have at least half as many different ones as you have students.

Procedure Tell students to envisage the following situation: They have an English speaking guest staying with them. Suddenly they hear something very exciting or interesting on the news or read something in the paper that makes them laugh or annoys them. Obviously the guest would like to know what the excitement, laughter, anger, etc. is about...

IV. Working with foreign language texts

Hand out the newspaper articles to one student.
Students sit in pairs. Give one of each pair a newspaper article. That student then reads his or her text without showing it to their partner. Afterwards they relate the essence of the article to their partner.

It should be made clear that students are not to translate verbatim. They should also cope with the task on their own without help from you.

Once students have finished paraphrasing their texts, hand out new ones to those who had to listen in the first round. Repeat the exercise with new texts if there is time.

3. One out of three

The common history of European languages is evident when you compare translations of the same sentence into three or more languages. The following exercise makes students aware of the fact that their knowledge of English can actually help them to understand texts in languages new to them.

As students will only have to guess individual words and the task is – on one level – so clearly above them, the game can be played from a post-beginner level onwards.

Preparation Make enough copies of the worksheet (page 72) for every student to have one.

Procedure Hand out the copies of the worksheet. Tell students that what they have on their pages is the same sentence expressed in three different languages. Their task will be to construct the English version from the material provided.

Students then read the three sentences and suggest words that may appear somewhere in the English texts.

If their guess is correct, tell them on which line they should write down the word.

As more and more words are found the structure of the sentence will become more apparent.

If students are stuck, you could give them a few clues by suggesting synonyms or pointing out unfinished structures that require a certain continuation.

Note that there might be more than one way to translate the given sentences into English. The objective here is, however, to find the *official* translation which can be found on page 72.

4. Translation with a difference

This exercise is a variation of *One out of three*. One of its aims is to show that a translation – even of a well understood text – does not necessarily follow the same word order as the original. This is why a mother tongue version of the target text can safely be provided without giving too much away. The other language provided in this exercise both gives further clues and can show similarities between itself and the target language or the students' mother tongue. This exercise can be done with pre-intermediate students and takes about ten minutes.

IV. Working with foreign language texts

Preparation Make enough copies of the worksheet for every student to have one (see page 73).

Procedure Hand out the worksheet. The task of the students is to find the English version of the Dutch and German texts printed on the worksheet. Students do this by suggesting words that they think will appear in the English text and the teacher then confirms or denies it. If the students guess correctly, the teacher will tell them on which line to write their word.

5. English – French – English

It is sometimes surprising how easily information can be gathered from a text written in a language one has never studied. This exercise trains the student in the picking up of information from a text written neither in the students' mother tongue nor in the target language of the course in which they are taking part. French is used here but other languages would be equally suitable. If for example one has the same brochure in various languages, one could let the students find out information from identical texts in, say, Dutch, Danish and Portuguese. The exercise presented here takes about fifteen minutes and can be done from a lower intermediate level upwards.

Preparation Make copies of the texts on page 74 and of the worksheet that goes with them (see page 75).

Procedure Hand out the two sheets of paper and let students find the answers to the questions on the worksheet. They can work in pairs or small groups. Careful reading is required as well as doing some arithmetic to transfer percentage figures into absolute figures. When everybody has completed the questionnaire, the results are discussed in class.

Variation On pages 75 and 76 another questionnaire and a collection of texts in French can be found.

The questions are based on an activity published in *Le Français dans le Monde, 1990*. The variation here is that the questions are in English rather than French.

Section V
Facts, texts and figures

Most games in this book do not require a great deal of knowledge of the EC. If, however, you want to do a teaching unit on the EC you will have to give students input. This section tries to show how this task can be made more stimulating than just handing out texts for homework or silent reading in the classroom.

It would go beyond the scope of this book to provide enough statistical and factual material for a whole teaching unit. The texts used in the following exercises are just examples and can by no means be representative. For up-to-date information turn to magazines and newspapers.

V. Facts, texts and figures

1. Europe by numbers

This game allows the teacher to feed some statistical information to the students in a communicative way. They will thus have material for group discussions that should lead to lively arguments. The game takes about fifteen minutes and can be played from an intermediate level upwards. Depending on the facts you provide, you might have to pre-teach some vocabulary.

For the worksheet to be used in this game, a good mixture of percentage figures, low figures and very high figures ensures that the game is not too demanding. If figures are too similar, student activity is reduced to random guesswork.

Preparation Prepare a worksheet of ten to twelve factual sentences that contain both relevant and trivial (but always correct) data on the Community or its individual countries, but with the figures in the sentences left out. A copiable sample can be found on page 77.

Procedure Organize students into groups of four.

Hand out the worksheets.

Tell them that they are working with real information on the EC.

Give them the numbers that are missing from the sentences in random order. You could either write them on the board or dictate them.

Ask students to match the numbers with the sentences.

When they have finished, discuss their solutions with the whole class and provide the correct answers.

2. The word rose

This exercise tries to raise expectations by letting students play around with a selection of words from the text they are going to read. As you can choose the words according to the level of your class, this exercise can be played from a post-beginner level onwards as long as the text fits.

Preparation Choose ten to fifteen words from the text you want to deal with in class. The words should not give away too much of the content.

Procedure Write the words you have chosen on the board in the shape of a word rose.

Example:

```
                        confusion
         responsibility                     words
              journalists                        police
       university                           misunderstandings
              tunnel                         conference
                 computers                 shades
                        telephone
```

V. Facts, texts and figures

Students then have to guess from the clues you have given what the text will be about.

It would also make sense to write down two words at a time and let students incorporate the new words into the context they imagine step by step.

The text from which these words have been taken can be found on page 77. Another set of words and a different text can be found on page 78.

3. Scrambled texts

This exercise helps students develop a feeling for the structure of English sentences. It can be done on most levels depending on the difficulty of the text you have chosen. The text used here would be for intermediate students. The exercise takes about ten minutes.

Preparation Select a short text you want students to work on. Type it up, leaving the lines intact but mixing up their order. Only the first and the last lines should be in their original position. Make copies of this newly arranged text.

Procedure Hand out copies of the jumbled text, tell the students what you have done and ask them to rearrange the lines into their original order. They should work in groups of three to five. They may ask you the meaning of any new words, but apart from that they should solve the task alone.

Examples of copiable texts can be found on page 79.

4. Euro diary

If the material you have is either too fragmented or too difficult for classroom use, there is a way in which you can adapt it to your students and feed them information in an interesting way at their level. What you have to do is put the information you want them to receive into the form of a diary entry. This allows you to slip in personal information as well. Let students share some reflections on your teaching and their learning and put in all sorts of comments of topical interest. What you end up with is reading material either for home study or classroom work. The drawback is, of course, that you have to write your own texts but then you can make use of all the mother tongue media information you can get hold of. You could also encourage your students to write such diary entries and present them to the class or to you to read.

To give you an idea of what such texts can look like there follow two excerpts of *Euro diary* entries which I once used in my class. No text for classroom use is reproduced in the appendix as this method is suitable only if adapted to the teacher's individual situation and to convey current information.

Preparation Collect pieces of information which you want your students to have. Combine them into a diary format, type them and make copies.

Procedure Bring the texts to class and hand out either as home study material or work on the texts in class.

V. Facts, texts and figures

Excerpts of 'Euro diary' entries:

> **October 27, 1989**
>
> The French seem to be afraid that the European Parliament might move to Brussels and leave Strasbourg. The British members seem to favour the Belgian capital and do not want to keep travelling between Brussels, Strasbourg and Luxembourg. So the French government wants to give every MEP a colour television with 21 channels, a personal fax machine and a bleeper which could send messages from anywhere in the EC. Some of the cost (which includes training the MEPs in how to use the machines) would be borne by the French government but more than £1 would still have to come from next year's European Community budget (...).

> **November 7, 1989**
>
> Can I ask my students to cut articles on the EC out of newspapers for me? Would they have the time? It was so easy in Britain: you open the paper and "Hey-presto!" you find a useful article on the EC.
> Understandably German papers are dominated by events in the GDR at the moment although you still find quite a number of articles on the EC. Many of them are, however, so technical that they really aren't suitable for the course. I mean, who wants to deal with the intricacies of the various systems of taxation in the EC countries? What good would it do them to know that VAT is either 6% or 12% in Spain, whereas in Germany the highest rate is 14% and in Italy it can go up to 38% (figures given in the "EG magazin"). It might be more interesting to know that VAT on books ranges from zero to seven per cent, except in Denmark where it is 22%! (...).

5. Cutting long stories short

If one deals with a topic like the EC in greater detail, it is inevitable that a fair amount of reading both inside and outside the classroom is necessary. This exercise makes the reading of texts less strenuous and more communicative. Depending on the text chosen, it can be adapted to most levels from pre-intermediate upwards and should take about ten to fifteen minutes.

Preparation Find a text with a lot of factual information and prepare a list of questions as you would for a regular reading comprehension exercise. Type these on a sheet of paper leaving enough space for students to fill in their answers.

Make a set of copies of the questions for the class.

Make copies of the original text and cut it up into small paragraphs, so that one snippet of paper gives the answer to one of the questions only. You should have as many snippets as you have students in the class.

V. Facts, texts and figures

Procedure Hand out the questionnaire – one per student. Then give each student one of the snippets of paper. Students then have to find the answers to all the questions on their worksheet. As from their one snippet they cannot possibly get all the information they need, they have to ask their classmates.

It is best to go through the questions one by one and let the class try and find the answer.

To deal with a long text on the European Parliament elections that appeared before the last election in 1989 I once used the following questionnaire:

> 1. How many members has the European Parliament got?
> 2. How many of them are British?
> 3. How many MEPs are women?
> 4. How many parties are represented in the EP?
> 5. Voting in Britain is different from voting in all other countries. In what way?
> 6. When will Portugal go to the polls?
> 7. Two countries will vote in national elections on the same day. Which ones?
> 8. When can the results of the elections be announced in Germany?
> 9. Three predictions are made about the outcome of the election. What are they?

The answers to the questions can be found in the following excerpts. The answers are *1–a, 2–b, 3–c,* and so on.

To get results quickly and correctly students have to

- do some well-pronounced reading of their bits of text to prove that they have got the answer
- clarify unknown words with the help of dictionaries or the teacher
- give and take dictation of the bits relevant to answering the questions
- rephrase the text to suit the questions.

This seems quite a complex set of skills – and the text used here is suitable for students who are at least on an upper-intermediate level. But this procedure is much more stimulating than the all too laborious working through one long text.

Example:

Large increase in the Green vote is expected

**From Michael Binyon
Strasbourg**

The 518 members of the European Parliament meet in their final session here tomorrow before dispersing to begin compaigning for the European elections next month.

With the quickening pace towards 1992, growing controversy over the future structure of the European Community and the increasingly visible role of the MEPs, public interest in the elections is at an all-time high, and in many Community states the results could have a significant domestic impact.

The elections establish a number of milestones as Europe gropes towards a federal democracy. It will be the first time that all 12 members of the enlarged Community vote at the same time. Mr David Steel's candidacy in the central region of Italy marks the first time that a senior politician from one country has stood for a constituency of another.

And it is the first time that MEPs will be campaigning for a Parliament that has been given considerably greater legislative and consultative powers since the signing of the Single European Act in 1987.

European elections are held every five years, and this is only the third time since 1979 that members have been directly elected. Previously MEPs were appointed from national Parliaments. Traditional polling days are retained in the 12 countries, so that five – Britain, Ireland, Denmark, Spain and The Netherlands – go to the polls on Thursday, June 15, while voters in the remaining seven will cast their ballots on Sunday, June 18. The results will not be announced in any country, including Britain, until after the last polls in Italy have closed on the Sunday evening at 9 pm BST!

The elections are not organized by the European Community or Parliament, but are held under the provisions of national legislation. An attempt in 1982 to create a uniform system of elections – as laid down in the basic Community treaties – failed to win agreement, so

> 'In many states, results could have a significant domestic impact'

this year, as before, each country will determine its own system.

That means that all, apart from Britain, will use a form of proportional representation, either using a "list" system of candidates or transferable votes.

British MEPs, however, like those in the House of Commons, will be the first-past-the-post winners in the 78 mainland constituencies, with the exception of the three Northern Ireland seats, which will use a single transferable vote.

In some countries EC citizens living in other member states may vote in their new homes, if the arrangement is reciprocal. Thus Irish citizens in Belgium can vote in Belgium and *vice versa*.

In Italy non-resident EC citizens can vote for the Italian lists and in The Netherlands they can do so only if they are ineligible to vote in their home states.

There are representatives of 79 different parties in the outgoing Parliament. The MEPs sit not in national groups but in nine political blocks. Some countries, such as Italy, have members from 12 different parties ranging from neo-fascist to Communist with members sitting in almost every political block.

The British MEPs are distributed among only four blocks: the European Democrats where the 45 Conservative MEPs are jointed by 17 conservatives from Spain and four from Denmark; the Socialist group, where 33 Labour Party members sit with socialists from every country except Ireland; the European Democratic Alliance where, Mrs Winifred Ewing, a Scottish Nationalist, is the lone British representative among 19 Gaullists, one Greek and eight Fianna Fail Irish MEPs; the European Right, which groups one Ulster Unionist – the Rev Ian Paisly – among 16 rightwingers, mostly French and Italian; and the Independents, where Mr John Hume represents the SDLP from Northern Ireland in a heterogeneous group of 15 MEPs who do not fit into any other category.

Of the outgoing members, 85 of the 518 are women, the largest group – 16 – coming from France. There were 12 women among the 81 British MEPs. The figure is likely to rise as many more women are standing for election. The Belgian Socialist Party list is headed by a woman, and Mme Catherine Trautman, the Mayor of Strasbourg, holds second place on the French Socialist Party list.

This year the European elections fall at a particularly sensitive time in many countries.

In two – Greece and Luxembourg – national elections are being held on the same day, and the campaign for the Strasbourg parliament will inevitably be overshadowed by the national contests.

In two other countries national

> 'The main change is likely to be a large increase in the Greens' share of the vote'

elections are due shortly afterwards: The Netherlands, where Mr Ruud Lubbers's Government has fallen and is continuing only as a caretaker administration, and in Spain, where Señor Felipe González is staking much on his current presidency of the European Community to boost the chances of a return to office for his Socialist Government. In Italy, the Government of Signor Ciriaco de Mita has just fallen and it is unclear whether there will be a new prime minister by June 18.

In West Germany the elections are seen as a crucial test for the shaky coalition of Chancellor Helmut Kohl and will, for the first time, turn largely on domestic issues. By contrast, in Britain the elections come as a mid-term referendum on Mrs Thatcher's Government but will probably focus more than at any other time on the issue of Europe.

The turnout will vary considerably. In several countries voting is compulsory, and in such places as Belgium and Luxembourg there was a 92 per cent and 89 per cent participation in 1984. In most other countries the turnout hovered between 50 and 70 per cent. It was lowest in Britain, at 33 per cent, although polls show an expected rise of at least 5 per cent this year.

The main change anticipated in the coming election is a large increase in the Green vote, reflecting the rise of environmental concerns throughout the Community.

The Greens, who sit as part of the "Rainbow Alliance" in the outgoing Parliament, have MEPs from only West Germany, Belgium and The Netherlands. But their numbers may increase, and in Britain,

(The Times, 25. 05. 1989)

V. Facts, texts and figures

a) The 518 members of the European Parliament meet in their final session here tomorrow before dispersing to begin campaigning for the European elections next month.

b) The elections are not organized by the European Community or Parliament but are held under the provisions of national legislation. An attempt in 1982 to create a uniform system of elections – as laid down in the basic Community treaties – failed to win agreement, so this year, as before, each country will determine its own system.

That means that all, apart from Britain, will use a form of proportional representation, either using a "list" system of candidates or transferable votes.

British MEPs, however, like those in the House of Commons, will be the first-past-the-post winners in the 78 mainland constituencies, with the exception of the three Northern Ireland seats, which will use a single transferable vote.

c) Of the outgoing members, 85 of the 518 are women, the largest group – 16 – coming from France. There were 12 women among the 81 British MEPs. The figure is likely to rise as many more women are standing for election. The Belgian Socialist Party list is headed by a woman, and Mme Catherine Trautman, the Mayor of Strasbourg, holds second place on the French Socialist Party list.

d) This year the European elections fall at a particularly sensitive time in many countries.

In two – Greece and Luxembourg – national elections are being held on the same day, and the campaign for the Strasbourg parliament will inevitably be overshadowed by the national contests.

e) There are representatives of 79 different parties in the outgoing Parliament. The MEPs sit not in national groups but in nine political blocks. Some countries, such as Italy, have members from 12 different parties ranging from neofascist to Communist with members sitting in almost every political block.

f) European elections are held every five years, and this is the third times since 1979 that members have been directly elected. Previously MEPs were appointed from national Parliaments. Traditional polling days are retained in the 12 countries, so that five – Britain, Ireland, Denmark, Spain and The Netherlands – got to the polls on Thursday, June 15, while voters in the remaining seven will cast their ballots on Sunday, June 18. The results will not be announced in any country, including Britain, until after the last polls in Italy have closed on the Sunday evening at 9 pm BST.

g) In West Germany the elections are seen as a crucial test for the shaky coalition of Chancellor Helmut Kohl and will, for the first time, turn largely on domestic issues. By contrast, in Britain the elections come as a midterm referendum on Mrs Thatcher's Government but will probably focus more than at any other time on the issue of Europe.

Section VI
A mixed bag

It is sometimes difficult to categorize games clearly. They either defy a meaningful classification or they combine various language learning activities. This section – by far the largest of this book – contains a collection of games that do not really fall into any of the other categories but are far too much fun to play to be left out of the book. Some of these games are classics adapted to an EC context. Others originated in the *Euro-classroom*. Together they show from how many different angles one topic can be approached and thus they should encourage the reader to add ideas of their own to the topic.

VI. A mixed bag

1. Which side are you on?

This activity gives students a chance to find fellow students who think alike on various subjects. It will also clarify where students stand on various European issues.

Preparation Select six to eight pairs of words which are taken out of a European context.

Example:

sandwich	–	baguette
Britain	–	Chunnel
Paris	–	Metro
Germany	–	Berlin
Belgium	–	Brussels
windmills	–	tulips
bobby	–	gendarme

Procedure Get students to stand in the middle of the classroom. Tell them they will have to make a choice about a number of pairs you are going to present to them. They should make their choice according to which of the two items they identify with. Tell them that they will have to opt for one or the other of the two items.

Call out the first pair, e.g. *sandwich – baguette*. Those who feel more attracted to *sandwich* should move to one side of the room, the *baguette people* should move to the other. Students then explain in pairs why they made their choices. Then students move to the other side of the room and talk to their opposites. This procedure is repeated for all the word pairs chosen.

The activity is a variation of *Forced choice* to be found in *Vocabulary* by *John Morgan* and *Mario Rinvolucri*.

2. Organising pairs: Words don't matter

Pair work should not be done with the same partner every time and getting students to remix is easy. The following exercise can be done from post-beginner level onwards and does not take more than five minutes. The format of the exercise allows students to *beat the system* and work together with the partner of their choice. All they have to do is come up with a clever reason why their cards match.

Preparation Select words you want to revise or choose words randomly. These should be nouns, adjectives or verbs. Write these words on small cards or slips of paper, one word per card. Make sure a large number of words have Euro connotations.

Procedure Hand out one card per student. Students then find a partner with a card that matches theirs. Matching can be done according to different criteria (perhaps provide examples such as: *Charles-Dickens, horse-bale of hay, The Netherlands-Amsterdam, sports car – expensive, Frankenstein – terrible, apple-tree – 'Apple' computer,* etc.). The choice of criteria is up to the students. Students then get up and mill around and if they are happy with the first word they meet they sit down together with the owner of that card. If they are not happy they move on. Once everyone has found their partners, get on with the pair work activity you had planned.

VI. A mixed bag

3. Find a European...

This classic game is modelled on Gertrude Moskowitz' *Search for someone who...* There are few games that rival it in liveliness and whole-class interaction. At the same time this game can be designed in such a way that it allows the students to practise one or two selected structures intensively. Having to get up brings some life into even the most exhausted group. The game can be adapted to any level from post-beginners onwards, and takes about ten to thirty minutes depending on the number and choice of questions. To make the questionnaire more interesting you could find out some unusual pieces of information about your students (that their fellow students will not know) beforehand and design the questionnaire accordingly.

Preparation Design a questionnaire similar to the one printed below and make enough copies for the whole of your class.

Example:

Name(s)	Find a European who...
1. Heike Peter	can say *Guten Tag* in more than three EC languages.
2.	has visited more than three EC capitals.
3. Meike	would like to learn Portuguese.
4. Tim	knows a Danish poet.
5. Anke Alex	has a pen-pal in an EC country.

A complete copiable questionnaire can be found on page 80.

Procedure Ask students to get up, mill around and interview their fellow students (*Do you...?, Have you...?*). When they get a *Yes*-answer they should ask that person to sign their name in the box provided. The game is finished when most people have completed the questionnaire.

To ensure that students do not just ask the person sitting next to them the following rule applies: No one is allowed to sign their names more than twice on one sheet.

4. Rain in Spain?

The following exercise may at first look like a geography test – and to some extent it is. But the main idea is to get students used to the way the names of European cities and towns are anglicized. The exercise does not take more than ten minutes and can be done from a post-beginner level upwards. A copiable text suitable for this exercise can be found on page 81.

VI. A mixed bag

Preparation Make enough copies of a weather chart (cut out of a newspaper) for each student to have one. The chart should also list a fair number of both European and other cities.

Procedure Students sit in groups of three to five and are handed the copied sheets of the weather chart. Their task is to identify in the list provided those cities and towns that are within EC countries. When they have finished let them compare their results in class.

5. Lucky thirteen

The following exercise can be done as a simple discussion of the question *Which country do you think should be allowed to join the EC next?* It can, however, be done in a more amusing style. The game is best played as a small group activity followed by a whole group phase. An intermediate level is required. The game takes a good half hour.

Preparation Write the names of some of the new applicants for EC-membership individually on slips of paper (e.g. Turkey, Sweden, Malta, Switzerland, Austria, etc.).

Procedure Organize students in groups of four or five. Let them pick one of the slips of paper (with the writing face down). Their task will be to argue for this country's membership of the EC. They should prepare for this in a group discussion which should not take longer than ten minutes. The other groups do the same with the country they picked.

Afterwards each group presents its case to the rest of the class, which raises further questions and counter-arguments.

In a large class one group may be made a jury to which the case has to be presented. While the other groups are preparing their statements, the jury devises questions and criteria on which to base its verdict.

6. My Belgium (or Portugal, Greece, etc.)

This exercise is most practical for courses that either repeatedly work on the EC or over a long period of time. It is mostly a homework exercise but can be turned into a communicative classroom activity as well. It is suitable at any level. No time limit can be given as this exercise can be extended over a longer time and at various intervals.

Procedure Ask students to choose a country they know very little about and put its name on top of one or more sheets of paper, prefixing it with *My* . . . . They should then write down what they do know about the country and collect information on that country from their classmates. Collecting information on this country will be an on-going homework task. Occasionally time should be set aside for students to share what they have found out with their classmates. This can be done in pairs or small groups. The material thus gathered can later be used in other games where more general knowledge is required.

VI. A mixed bag

7. If butter montains were real

Butter mountains and wine lakes have been one of the negative features of EC agricultural policy for years. In this exercise they are turned to a new use: to practise conditionals. This game can therefore be played as soon as the relevant structure has been taught and as soon as students command a basic vocabulary. The game takes about fifteen minutes.

Procedure Write the sentence *If butter mountains were real...* on the board. Then ask students to find as many endings to this sentence as possible. Instead of butter mountains you could use sugar mountains, oil lakes, wine lakes, etc. When students have finished writing about three to eight sentences each, ask them to read them out to the class.

VI. A mixed bag

8. Demonstrations

This game can lead to a lively discussion of current affairs or a light-hearted exchange of nonsensical ideas. In a small class it can be done as a whole group exercise, in a large class it should be done in groups of four to six. Allow about half an hour for this game so that students can not only present their own views but also comment on those of the other students. It can be played at and above an intermediate level.

Procedure Mention the fact that many people have a pet gripe about which they feel strongly: noise, traffic, cruelty to animals, fast food, incorrect use of the apostrophe, etc. Then ask them what they would like to demonstrate against if they were given the money to transport 10,000 people from different EC countries to Brussels or any of the other European capitals in order to demonstrate against something. They should also come up with one or two slogans that would be found on the posters or banners to be carried around during the demonstration. To be meaningful the demonstration should not be directed against a local grievance but something that (at least some) people from all countries could protest against.

9. Oh, what a night!

This is a pair-work exercise that allows students to share some of their personal experience in EC countries. It can be played from an intermediate level upwards and takes about fifteen minutes.

Procedure Ask students to list three places in which they have spent one night. The places should, of course, be within the EC and ideally be related to a memorable, unusual or at least new experience. They should then share their memories of these three places with their partners. In small groups one could ask for the most memorable experience to be told to the whole class.

10. All around Europe

This is a fast-paced and lively game that gets all the students talking about their own memories of Europe, current European affairs or other things they know about the various EC countries. It can be played from intermediate level upwards and takes about twenty to thirty minutes.

Procedure Split the class into two groups and get students to sit in two circles, an inner circle facing outwards and an outer circle facing inwards, so that you end up with pairs of students facing each other.

Students write down the names of any six of the twelve EC countries on a sheet of paper. (No particular order required.)

Students then declare the first country from their list and tell their partner what memories/associations/knowledge they have regarding that particular country; e.g.: *Greece is one of the two EC countries I've never been to. I don't know why, really. I think the reason is that...* or *I've been to Luxembourg three times. Once was only for a short trip – a walk round the capital, a cup of coffee. Come to think of it, I've never been on my own in Luxembourg. The first time a friend took me to Luxembourg airport to catch a plane to the USA. The second time...*

VI. A mixed bag

They then listen to what their partners have to say about the first country on their list.

Once they have finished that exchange, one circle moves on to a neighbouring chair, so that everybody has a new partner. Everybody now takes the second country from their list and strikes off the one he or she has already talked about. This is repeated until all six countries have been talked about.

Keep it fast-paced. Students should not have time to run out of things to say. They should be forced to relate their stories quickly. If the group likes this activity there is no reason why you should not go on to do all twelve countries.

11. European treasure chest

This exercise focuses on vocabulary. The main objective is to identify and revise words the students already know. The exercise is thus suitable for all levels from post-beginners to advanced. It can be done as homework, in pairs, in small groups or as a whole class activity. The procedure is very simple. The exercise takes about fifteen minutes. Warning: The map of Europe used in this game is very stereotyped!

Preparation Bring to class copies of the map of Europe on page 82.

Procedure Hand out copies of the map of Europe – one per student or per pair of students.

Ask students to name as many items pictured on the map as they can. They should write down the words on the lines provided. If they are not sure about the spelling they should ask you or consult their neighbours.

When they have finished, go through the vocabulary with the whole class. To make the exercise more manageable ask for *food-words*, *holiday-words* or words beginning with *w* rather than all the words in the exercise.

To make students scan their collections again you could also ask questions like *What can one find in Britain?* or *Where do you see the windmills?*.

Variation Make two different copies of the map. Blank out different items on each with Tipp-Ex. Ask students to find the differences.

You could add to this collection of words by asking for further things typical of or produced in a certain country.

As the map is so stereotyped ask for things that are missing from it and discuss whether students feel their country is adequately represented.

VI. A mixed bag

12. A language learning loop

Many students are reluctant to admit it when they have not understood something and may also have difficulties in producing question forms accurately. The following text deals with these problems head-on: to understand the text itself, the students will probably have to ask a number of questions. The content of the text reflects the psychological problem of asking questions and provides sentence models for doing so in a grammatically correct way. The insight the text provides can immediately be put into practice by asking questions. The mental problem is thus identical with the linguistic task.
The exercise takes about fifteen minutes. The version of the text presented on page 83 is meant for intermediate students.

The idea of *loops* i.e. the content of the activity referring to the activity itself can be found explained in *Loop-input* by *Tessa Woodwards*.

Preparation Copy the text on page 83 or a variation of it that is better suited to the competency of your students.

Procedure Hand out copies of the text.

Do not tell the students what is special about the text or why you are dealing with it.

Read out the text loud at normal speed but pause briefly after each sentence so that the contents can sink in and students have a chance to ask questions.

When you have finished reading it out wait for students to ask questions.

13. Memories of English

English is the most widely used lingua franca. Students are almost certain to have used English to communicate with non-English people during holidays or in their job. The following activity can be played from intermediate level upwards. It could be used as a lead-in to a discussion of the language problem in the EC / in Europe. The exercise takes about twenty minutes.

Procedure Ask students to write down in telegram style as many Europeans as they can remember with whom they have communicated with in English during their lives. They should, however, list only those people to whom English was not the mother tongue.

Example:

> Portuguese hotelier
> Swedish bank clerk
> Italian hitch-hiker
> Ghanaian immigrant
> Belgian policeman
> Portuguese employee of car rental agency
> French waiter

VI. A mixed bag

Dictate the beginning of this sentence:

I have used English in Europe to communicate with...

Students then share their lists with other students in groups of three. They should however, not just read the lists, but convey some more information about the various situations.

14. Shopping for Europe

This board game gives students the chance to be creative and use their knowledge of EC affairs. The game is best played in groups of four to six students at or above intermediate level. It takes about thirty minutes. A copiable version of a board can be found on page 84.

This is a variation of a game I learned from *Frank Steele*.

Preparation Cut pictures of objects out of magazines. You should have a good mixture of everyday objects as well as unusual ones (a food processor, a steamroller, an elephant, etc.). Stick these onto postcard-size cards or pieces of paper. Have dice and markers ready.

Procedure Tell students that they should pretend they are working for a company the characteristics of which they should make up themselves individually and write down: a) the product or service b) number of employees c) anything else they find important.

Tell them that they have all bought something for the firm without authorization. They bought it, because they could get it at a bargain price and because they thought it would be useful for the firm especially with respect to the Single European Market.

Let students form groups of four to six. Then hand out a board like the one presented on page 84. Let students choose markers.

Give each student three picture cards, each one showing an object bought. If you have not got enough pictures, you could always write the name of the object on the card.

Students take turns in rolling a dice and then move their markers accordingly. Whenever a student lands on one of the marked fields he or she chooses one of his or her picture cards and has to argue why this is a useful investment for the firm. The rest of the group try to argue against it. If the student can convince them, she or he is allowed to move ahead three fields and put down one of the cards. If not, she or he stays in the same place and keeps the card as well.

Students need to reach *Finish* to win. They need the exact number of points to be allowed to move into the last field. Should students find themselves past the last marked field without having got rid of all their cards, they have to move back to the last marked field.

The winner is, of course, the student who has got rid of all cards and reaches *FINISH* first.

VI. A mixed bag

15. My Place – the Video

The following exercise should perhaps best be done as a homework project. The amount of time it takes depends on the students. The level is lower intermediate and upwards.

The results of the students' work could be presented photocopied onto OHP transparency or as photocopies on paper. If you want to copy the students' storyboards, let students know beforehand what kind of colours your copier can read.

This homework project could run throughout the course with one or two presentations per lesson. You could copy the video sheet onto transparencies and give a set of pens to one or two students per week.

Preparation Copy enough storyboards to hand out to the students (see page 85).

Procedure Ask students to design a video on the place where they live. The text should, of course, be written in the language they are studying. The story-board sheets provided ask students to invent the pictures as well as the commentary.

The video could serve to achieve one of several objectives:

- to prove that your village / town / city / region is a truly European one
- to deter people from coming to your area because you do not want more traffic passing in front of your home
- to encourage people from a given EC country to come to your area because it is either totally different from or very similar to what they are used to.

Students might want to find their own theme. It should, however, be somehow connected with the EC.

In the next lesson students present their storyboards to the class.

16. What if...?

This exercise has a grammar focus (conditionals) so the relevant structures will have to be taught first. The exercise should take about thirty minutes and can be played with intermediate students.

Procedure Students form two groups.

Group A writes as many sentences as they can, starting with *What if...?*

Examples:

- What if Britain were to leave the EC?
- What if the Single Market does not work?
- What if everybody had to learn the same language?

Group B then writes down answers to the questions they suppose Group A will come up with.

The students of Group A then read out their questions in turn, Group B students take turns answering.

Then the students of Group B read out the answers they have prepared for the supposed questions of Group A. Group A must then find the questions to the answers of Group B. For each answer they can try three times to find the correct question.

Again students take turns doing this. If the first attempt does not succeed, the guessing passes on to the next student.

If this game is played competitively each correct question / answer is awarded one point.

17. Euro party

Having to give speeches, even brief ones on a topic, can put quite a strain on students. The following game makes this task much easier. The game can be played from lower intermediate level upwards because students prepare their own *texts*. The game takes about fifteen minutes.

Preparation Set students the following homework:
Find some news item/s in your paper that deal(s) with the EC and be prepared to talk about it/them in English in the next class.

Procedure Get students to stand up and stand around in cocktail party fashion. Introduce one of the students to another by saying e.g. *Mary, this is Robert. I'm sure you've got a lot to talk about. He's also very interested in EC affairs*. Repeat this with the other students until everybody is talking.

If students do not start mixing on their own, gently interrupt the pairs and bring students into contact with someone new.

18. My European paradise park

Theme parks cater for a majority taste rather than individual ones. This exercise asks students to list not the *official* major attractions of Europe but their own ones. The exercise takes about fifteen minutes and is suitable from a lower intermediate level upwards.

Procedure Mention theme parks and amusement parks like Disneyland or Legoland and ask students to design their own ideal park.

The park should contain as many features as possible that represent their ideal Europe. This could range from replicas of certain buildings, to a certain type of restaurant or shop or a particular landscape. They make notes of some of these features or even draw a map of the park and then share them with a partner.

19. EURO-whatsits

The more our lives are affected by EC regulations the more often we read about *EURO this* and *EURO that* in the newspapers. This short game works equally well with students who have some knowledge of EC affairs and those who do not. It can be played from a post-beginner level upwards and takes ten to fifteen minutes.

VI. A mixed bag

Procedure Ask students to give you about fifteen to twenty random nouns in their plural forms.

Write these all over the board.

Finally write the prefix *Euro* in the middle of the board.

Students then discuss in pairs in what way prefixing their words with *Euro* could make sense.

Example:

```
                    dogs
        countries           microprocessors
    friends                           accidents
sausages             Euro                    flowers
    Englishmen                        kilometres
        smells              screws
                    Indians
```

20. We are the world – We are Europe

This exercise is – like *Find a European* – ideal for students getting to know one another. It also creates a lively atmosphere. It can be played from an intermediate level upwards and takes about fifteen to thirty minutes.

Preparation Bring a world map and a map of Europe to class. Prepare two sheets, one saying *We are the world* the other saying *We are Europe*. You will also need cards or pieces of A6 paper – about five per student. Different coloured cards will look livelier later on but are not essential.

Procedure Put the world map up on a wall. Above the map put the sheet with the words *We are the world*. Put the map of Europe next to it. Above it put the sheet with the words *We are Europe*.

Hand out the cards or sheets of A6 paper to students. Students write the following sentence beginnings on the top of their cards – one sentence per card:

A. Someone in this room...

B. Someone in this room has...

C. Someone in this room has got...

(The ratio should be A = 5, B = 4 and C = 1.)

Students get up, mill around and briefly interview their fellow students for things that are (or they think are) *unique* about them. Provide some examples about yourself.

VI. A mixed bag

Examples:

> I think I'm the only person in this room
> • who has got three sisters and one brother
> • who was swum in the Niagara River
> • who in 1989 dented a policeman's car in Lisbon.

They collect information and complete the sentences on their cards. The following rules apply: A-sentences must not continue with *has* or *has got* and B-sentences must not continue with *got* or *a/an*.

Each completed card should then be put on the wall round the world map or the map of Europe (provide thumb tacks, Sellotape or other appropriate material). Only the cards relating to a European country or European affairs should go around the map of Europe. Once all cards are used up, get students to look at the complete collection of cards and read them.

If you can leave the cards on the wall, students will usually come back to them later in order to find out who the people behind the cards are.

A trial run in a teacher training seminar once yielded the following results:

> Someone in this room has been to India a lot of times.
> Someone in this room celebrates her birthday on December 24.
> Someone in this room saw Prince Charles last summer.
> Someone in this room has gambled in Las Vegas.
> Someone in this room used to live on a houseboat on the Thames.
> Someone in this room has travelled 10,000 miles across the USA.
> Someone in this room has seen *Pygmalion* at Covent Garden.
> Someone in this room once went on a cycling-tour through Germany.
> Someone in this room has successfully participated in a triathlon.
> Someone in this room breeds dogs.
> Someone in this room listens to the BBC almost every morning.
> Someone in this room has got a tattoo on his belly.
> Someone in this room has been to Cairo.
> Someone in this room knows Russian and Polish.

21. Identity cards

This pair work exercise gives students a chance to talk at their own pace about their relationships with some European aspects. The exercise works well from an intermediate level upwards and takes about fifteen to twenty minutes.

Procedure Ask students to take a sheet of paper and write their names in the middle. Then ask them to write the following pieces of information in the four corners of the sheet:

VI. A mixed bag

Example:

One, two or more EC capitals you've visited		One or two first names of friends you have in EC countries
	Name	
The EC country you know least about		An EC country you'd like to visit

Then pair them off, ask them to exchange sheets and let them explain what they have written down.

22. Don't go to prison! Collect 400 ECUs!

This game is rather more involved with the personal preferences, hobbies and perhaps political views of students than with the EC, but it still gets them to focus on the various EC countries. The game can be played in pairs or small groups. It takes ten to twenty minutes at intermediate level.

Procedure   Mention the fact that prisons in many EC countries are overcrowded. European integration on the citizen level is still lacking. Imagine that the EC has therefore ruled that prison sentences for some offences (e.g. those against the environment) must be EC based whilst others may be exchanged against an EC based punishment. The offender has to do six months *Community Service* (in the widest sense of the word) in another EC country. To promote the scheme people who voluntarily convert their prison term into Community Service will get 400 ECUs at the end of their period of service.

Students now list three such services they would *gladly* accept and three they would detest. They then exchange their choices with their partners.

23. Choose your own topic

One of the problems in conversation courses is that almost everybody who takes part is interested in a different topic. Finding a common denominator is difficult and often leads to the choice of a topic that hardly anybody is really interested in.

The following game tries to overcome this problem by giving students the chance to talk about either one topic in detail or a lot of topics superficially. Which topic they go into a greater length is up to them.

Preparation   Choose about ten sentences that have come connection with Europe. They can be trivia or more serious political matter. The sentences should be roughly at the language level of your students i.e. not require much explanation.

Type these sentences on a sheet of paper and intersperse them with other sentences, such as graffiti, proverbs, nonsense, sentences you might have found in novels and liked, etc. A useful number is twelve to twenty sentences.

VI. A mixed bag

Make copies for each student.

Depending on the choice of sentences this game can be played from a lower intermediate level onwards and can take fifteen to thirty minutes. Sentences with a European content can be found in any newspaper. A sample worksheet can be found on page 86. All *Euro-sentences* on that worksheet were taken from one copy of *THE EUROPEAN* (6–8 December 1991).

Procedure Students sit in pairs. Give each student the sheet with the collection of sentences. Tell them that they should discuss the sentences between them in the order in which they appear on the page; when they feel they have exhausted a sentence they should move on to the next one. Emphasize that they should tackle one sentence at a time and not read the whole page before starting to talk.

24. European love affair

This exercise allows students to do some creative writing. As songs often have fairly simple lyrics, this task should not be too demanding and can thus already be done at a lower intermediate level. The exercise might best be done as homework, as thinking up the words to a song can be time-consuming.

Procedure Hand out or project the following chorus of a song:

> I need some
> Italian wine,
> some German beer,
> and a glass of French champagne,
> some good Scotch whisky,
> some British gin and
> a Russion vodka to ease my pain.
> I need a Greek ouzo, and a Spanish sherry,
> and a pint of Irish ale,
> 'cos I just had another disastrous European love affair.
> (The text of the chorus was written by *Jeff Mezzrow*.)

Ask students to suggest meanings to the phrase *European love affair*.

They then go about writing one or two verses to precede this chorus.

Afterwards they read out their own texts to the class.

Useful contact addresses

A wide range of publications is available both from the

> Office for official publications of the European Communities in
> L-2985 Luxembourg

as well as from the

> Commission of the European Communities
> Publications Division
> Rue de la Loi 200
> B-1049 Bruxelles

The offices of the Commission of the European Communities in the twelve member states also provide a lot of brochures and are a good source of foreign language material. Sometimes even posters and videos are available.

Here is a list of the main offices:

Belgium

> a) Commission des Communautés européennes
>   Bureau en Belgique
> b) Commissie van de Europese Gemeenschappen
>   Bureau in België
> Rue Archimède 73, B-1049 Bruxelles
> Archimedesstraat 73, B-1049 Brussel

Denmark

> Kommissionen for De Europæiske Fællesskaber
> Kontor i Danmark
> Højbrohus
> Østergade 61
> Postbox 144
> DK-1004 København K

France

> Commission des Communautés européennes
> Bureau de représentation en France
> 288, boulevard Saint-Germain
> F-75007 Paris

Germany

> Kommission der Europäischen Gemeinschaften
> Vertretung in der Bundesrepublik Deutschland
> Zitelmannstraße 22
> D-5300 Bonn

Greece

> Επιτροπή των Ευρωπαϊκών Κοινοτήτων
> Γραφείο στην Ελλάδα
> 2 Vassilissis Sofias
> Postfach 11002
> Athina 10674

Ireland

> Commission of the European Communities
> Office in Ireland
> Jean Monnet Centre
> 39 Molesworth Street
> Dublin 2

Italy

> Commissione delle Comunità europee
> Ufficio in Italia
> Via Poli 29
> 00187 Roma

Luxembourg

> Commission des Communautés européennes
> Bureau au Luxembourg
> Bâtiment Jean Monnet
> Rue Alcide De Gasperi
> L-2920 Luxembourg

Contact addresses

Portugal

Comissão das Comunidades Europeias
Gabinete em Portugal
Centro Europeu Jean Monnet
Largo Jean Monnet 1-10º
P-1200 Lisboa

Spain

Comisión de las Comunidades Europeas
Oficina en España
Calle de Serrano 41, 5.ª planta
E-28001 Madrid

The Netherlands

Commissie van de Europese
Gemeenschappen
Bureau in Nederland
Korte Vijverberg 5
2513 AB Den Haag

The United Kingdom

Commission of the European Communities
Office in the United Kingdom
Jean Monnet House
8, Storey's Gate
London SW1 P3AT

Some countries have more than one office. The addresses of these can usually be found at the back of brochures published by the Commission.

For publications in English on the European Parliament write to:

UK Information Office of the
European Parliament
2 Queen Anne's Gate
London SW1H 9AA

Other sources:

Council of Europe
Avenue de L'Europe
F-67006 Strasbourg-Cedex

European Court of Human Rights
Palais de L'Europe
F-67006 Strasbourg

In Germany the following institutions and organisations can also be approached for information:

Informationsbüro des Europäischen Parlaments
Bundeskanzlerplatz,
Bonn-Center
5300 Bonn 1

Rat der Gemeinden Europas
Deutsche Sektion
Kaiserswerther Str. 199–201
4000 Düsseldorf 30

Europa-Union Deutschland
Generalsekretariat
Bachstraße 32
5300 Bonn 1

Deutscher Rat der Europäischen Bewegung e.V.
Generalsekretariat
Bachstraße 32
5300 Bonn 1

Bibliography

I have attended quite a few of *Mario Rinvolucri's* teacher training seminars and have read almost all of his books. Many of the ideas presented in *Totally EUROtic* have been inspired by him or by books written by his colleagues. For further excellent ideas, readers who like these games should consult the books mentioned in the following list. Many more useful titles can be found in the bibliographies of these books.

1. John Morgan and Mario Rinvolucri. *Vocabulary*.
   Oxford 1986 (Oxford University Press)

2. Gertrude Moskowitz. *Caring and Sharing in the Foreign Language Class*.
   Rowley, Mass. 1978: Newbury House

3. Tessa Woodward. *Loop-input. A set of strategies designed to help language teacher trainers and teachers' self-help groups to add variety to training sessions*.
   Canterbury 1988

4. David A. Hill. *Visual Impact. Creative language learning through pictures*.
   Harlow 1990: Pilgrims/Longman

5. Paul Davis and Mario Rinvolucri. *Dictation. New methods, new possibilities*.
   Cambridge 1988 (Cambridge University Press)

6. Randal Holme. *Talking texts. Innovative recipes for intensive reading*.
   Harlow 1991: Pilgrims/Longman

II. Working with pictures and cartoons

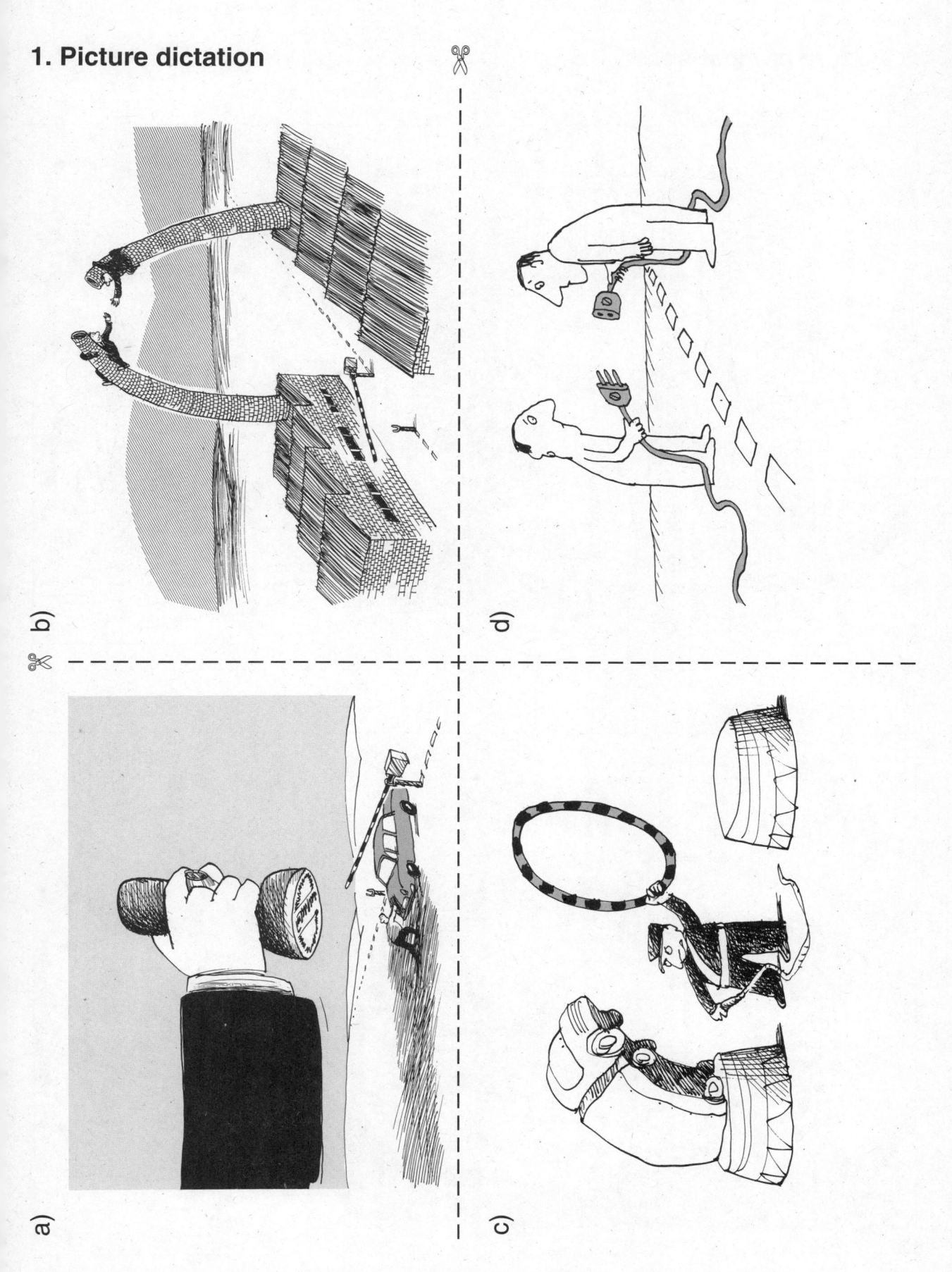

1. Picture dictation

II. Working with pictures and cartoons

2. Picture comparison I

A

B

II. Working with pictures and cartoons C

2. Picture comparison I (alternative)

A

B

C   II. Working with pictures and cartoons

3. Picture comparison II

A

II. Working with pictures and cartoons

3. Picture comparison II

B

II. Working with pictures and cartoons

3. Picture comparison II

Empty frames for the teacher's own material.

II. Working with pictures and cartoons

4. The bonfire

Solution:

"IT'S THE E.C. THEY WANT YOU TO PUT OUT YOUR BONFIRE"

(The Guardian 1991)

(The Guardian 1991)

6. Cartoons as a puzzle

(Daily Mail, 31.07.1989)

II. Working with pictures and cartoons

6. Cartoons as a puzzle

(Daily Mail, 31.07.1989)

✂ -

Holiday air cash chaos

SPAIN 'THE ONLY TYPHOID LINK'

BRITISH health officials have dismissed a Spanish claim that there is no outbreak of typhoid in the country.

The Health Department has said that with five typhoid cases among British holidaymakers to the Costa Dorada resort of Salou, the only common factor was their holiday.

Madrid's Ministry of Health last night gave an assurance to the British Embassy that nobody was being treated for the diseases in its hospitals.

But British officials insisted: 'Irrespective of what the Spanish are saying, the only common denominator is that these people holidayed in Salou.'

By PAUL MAURICE
Air Correspondent

A CASH row yesterday threatened travel plans of hundreds of holiday-makers.

Paramount Airways temporarily refused to let four of its planes fly while it demanded payments from four tour companies.

The Bristol-based airline, which carries 25,000 holidaymakers a week, is insisting that tour companies pay charter fees four weeks in advance.

It ordered four of its aircraft, scheduled to carry more than 500 holidaymakers, not to take off from Birmingham, Manchester, Newcastle and Belfast airports.

Five hundred more tourists waiting in Greece, Spain and Cyprus were warned that their aircraft might be 'indefinitely' delayed. But in the end only flights from Manchester to Greece and from Belfast to Spain were held for a couple of hours while the wrangle was temporarily resolved. Paramount claimed that the tour operators — Owners Abroad, Air 2000, Intersun and Redwing — had failed to pay a month in advance for the flights under the terms of their contract. Later Paramount chairman Jack Mario Berry, elected to the board only last week, allowed the aircraft back into the air.

'We realised that the passengers must come first,' he said. 'We will keep flying until further notice.'

Errol Cossey, managing director of Air 2000, denied owing Paramount money. 'Overall, I reckon they in fact owe me money,' he claimed.

Robert Smart, planning director of the International Leisure Group, owners of Intersun, said 'a commercial dispute' was caused by a change in the ownership of the airline. Paramount was sold last week to a company called Laneley 51.

(Daily Mail, 03.08.1989)

II. Working with pictures and cartoons

7. Look, no words!

a)

b)

c)

II. Working with pictures and cartoons

7. Look, no words!

e)

f)

d)

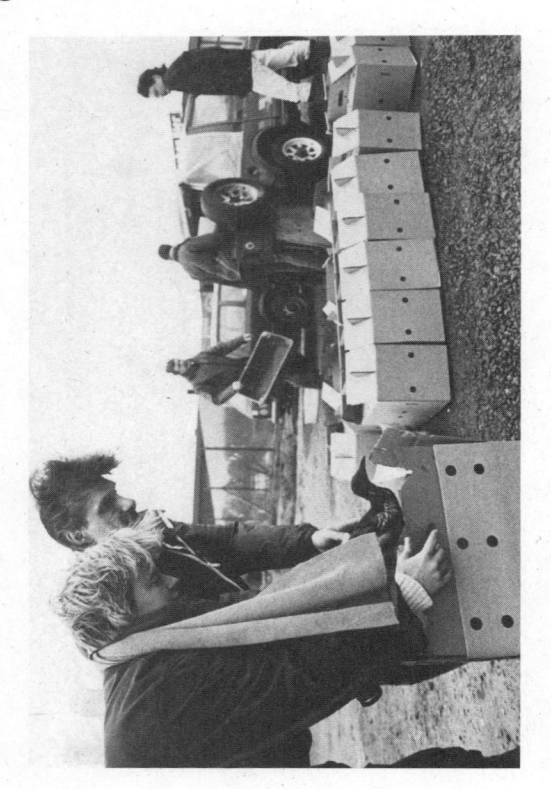

15. Picture associations

a)
London

PERCY WHELAN sleeps on several layers of cardboard in a subway under Waterloo Bridge. He wakes up before dawn each morning, a habit left over from his fishing days on the Irish Sea. Percy, who hasn't slept in a bed since he lost his job as a barman three years ago, is 59 in June and reckons it is about time he "retired", though it is hard to see how that would change his lifestyle. Each morning he has a hot shower and a meal at the Manna Centre near London Bridge. He spends the rest of his day "messing around, keeping his eye on things".

He rarely goes hungry, and seems remarkably unconcerned about the precariousness of his situation. But things would be a lot harder, he says, without the commitment of charities. Percy deplores begging, even though it could provide a hefty supplement to the £79 ($142) in benefit which he receives fortnightly. Most of that he spends immediately on drink at the nearest off-licence - anything left over goes on gambling on horse-racing at the bookie's.

Michael Bond

(The European, 05.11.1992)

b)
Berlin

DIETER KÜHN has been living on the streets since he swapped life under communism for the freedom of the West. He said: "I was thrown out of East Germany in September 1988 for being politically unacceptable.

"They fixed me up with a flat in West Berlin, but it was too expensive and I couldn't get work. Since then I've had nowhere to go. I was divorced before I left East Berlin and my wife won't help now."

Kühn sleeps on a park bench. "It's dangerous. I've had my fingers and a leg broken by attackers. But at least then I get to spend some time in hospital, where it's warm and there's plenty of food."

Julia Stone

(The European, 05.11.1992)

IV. Working with foreign language texts

1. What language? (a - g)

a)

Pensez-vous que la création du grand marché européen sera pour vous personnellement :

en %	une bonne chose	une mauvaise chose	une chose ni bonne ni mauvaise
RFA	28,8	6	60,3
Belgique	47,4	6	45,7
Danemark	40,1	12,1	47,6
Espagne	50,9	5,6	43,4
France	45,5	9,7	45,1
Royaume-Uni	53,3	9,2	33,3
Grèce	50	5,6	41,3
Irlande	74	11	14
Italie	72	3	21,6
Luxembourg	28,2	5,1	66,6
Pays-Bas	34,5	8,2	57,3
Portugal	57	1,5	22,6

(PHOSPHORE Nr.96, BAYARD PRESSE, 1989)

b) Ny samarbejdsprocedure med Europa-Parlamentet

EF-KOMMISSIONEN — Forslag
EUROPA-PARLAMENTET — 1.høring
MINISTERRÅDET — Foreløbig stilling med kvalificeret flertal
EUROPA-PARLAMENTET — 2.høring (ingen ændring / ændrings forslag / afvisende holdning)
EF-KOMMISSIONEN
MINISTERRÅDET — Endelig vedtagelse med kvalificeret flertal / Endelig vedtagelse med kvalificeret flertal*) / Endelig vedtagelse med enstemmighed

*) Afvigelser fra EF-Kommissionens forslag er **kun** mulig med enstemmighed.

Første tre måneders frist / En måneds frist / Anden tre måneders frist

c)

PROGRAMAS DE TELEVISIÓN

Viernes 18
19,47 Redacción de noche.
20,35 Polideportivo.
20,50 Clásicos del cine mudo: „El precio de la gloria"
23,00 Tribuna internacional.

Sábado 19
15,32 Retrato en vivo.
16,30 Barbapapá.
17,00 Dick Turpin.
17,30 Retransmisión deportiva.
19,00 La clave: „OTAN".

Domingo 20
18,45 La música.
20,00 Los últimos años del cine español.
22,00 La danza.
22,30 A fondo.

d) Bakai·Keller·Takács
Motorosok segédmotorosok tankönyve
Vizsgafelkészítő
Műszaki Könyvkiadó

e) FRANKRIJK
Bevolking : 55.996.000 inwoners
Oppervlakte : 551.695 km²
Hoofdstad : Parijs
Staatsvorm : De Vijfde Franse Republiek is een constitutionele republiek met aan het hoofd een president, die voor zeven jaar gekozen wordt. De wetgevende macht is in handen van de Assemblée Nationale en de Senaat.

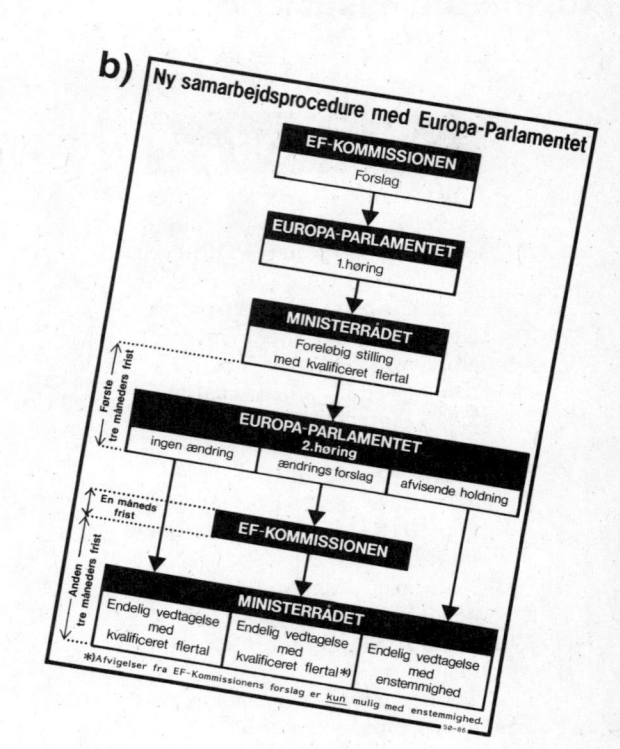

f) TRE DOLĈE SUR LAGO

Tre dolĉe glitadas boato
Vespere sur lago spegula;
Kaj akvo sub ĉiu rembato
Sulkiĝas kun sono regula.

Tre dolĉe forpasas minutoj
Sur ŝipo solece trankvila;
Nur voĉo mallaŭta de flutoj
Alflugas tra l' nokto lunbrila.

Tre dolĉe la flutoj sonĝigas...
Boato fariĝas gondolo;
La lumoj de l' bordo briligas
Palacojn sub fea kupolo.

Tre dolĉe revivas mi horon
De nokt' sub itala ĉielo;
Sed perdis ĉielo la gloron,
Ĉar nun al ĝi mankas anĝelo.

g)

な na	に ni	ぬ nu	ね ne	の no
は ha(wa)	ひ hi	ふ fu	へ he(e)	ほ ho

Solution: a) French b) Danish c) Spanish d) Hungarian
e) Dutch f) Esperanto g) Japanese

IV. Working with foreign language texts

1. What Language? (h - n)

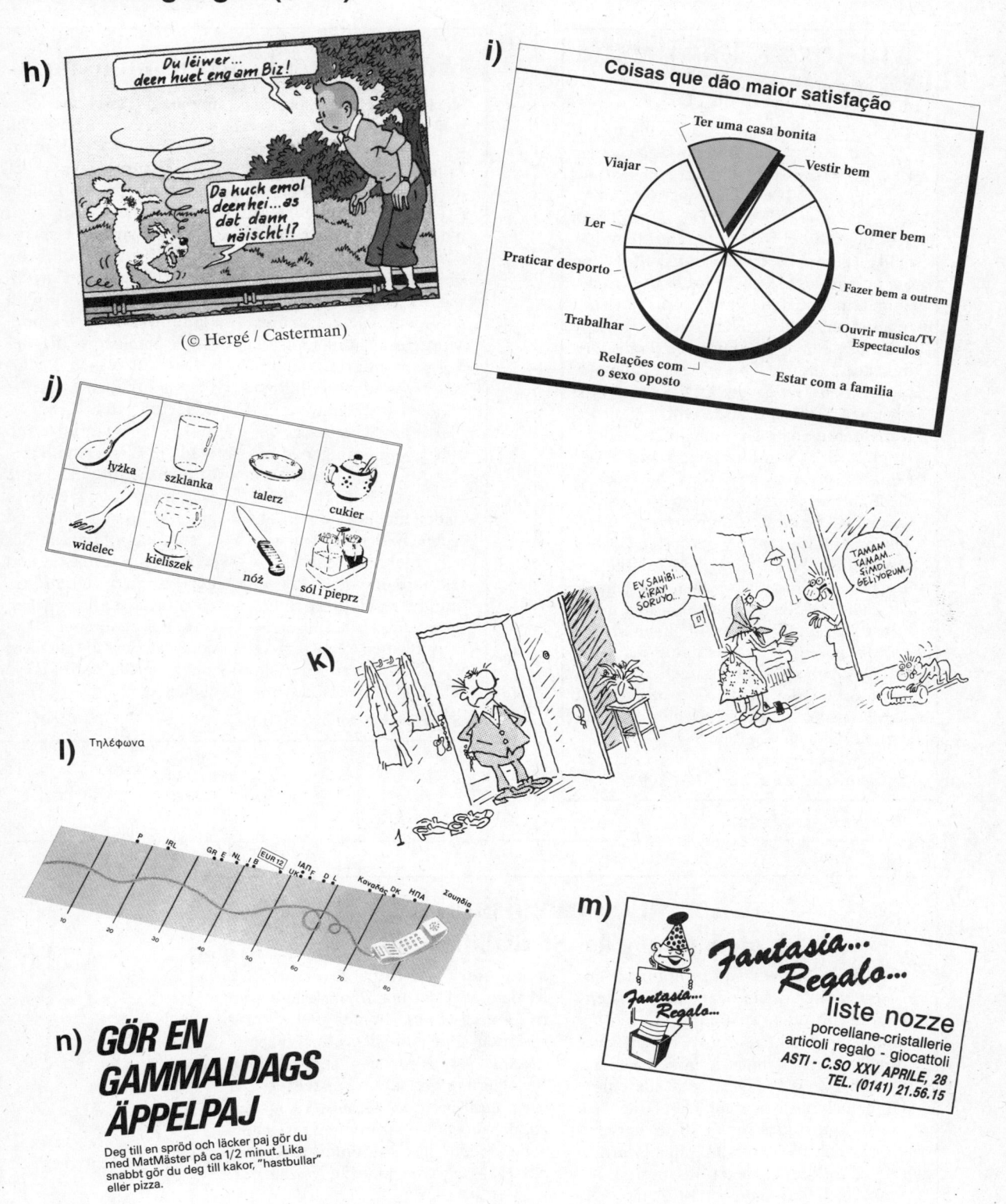

h) "Du léiwer... deen huet eng am Biz!" / "Da kuck emol deen hei... as dat dann näischt!?"
(© Hergé / Casterman)

i) Coisas que dão maior satisfação
- Ter uma casa bonita
- Vestir bem
- Comer bem
- Fazer bem a outrem
- Ouvrir musica/TV Espectaculos
- Estar com a familia
- Relações com o sexo oposto
- Trabalhar
- Praticar desporto
- Ler
- Viajar

j) łyżka, szklanka, talerz, cukier, widelec, kieliszek, nóż, sól i pieprz

k) "EV SAHIBI... KIRAYI SORUYO." / "TAMAM TAMAM... ŞIMDI GELIYORUM."

l) Τηλέφωνα

m) Fantasia... Regalo...
liste nozze
porcellane-cristallerie
articoli regalo - giocattoli
ASTI - C.SO XXV APRILE, 28
TEL. (0141) 21.56.15

n) GÖR EN GAMMALDAGS ÄPPELPAJ
Deg till en spröd och läcker paj gör du med MatMäster på ca 1/2 minut. Lika snabbt gör du deg till kakor, "hastbullar" eller pizza.

Solution: h) Letzeburgesch   i) Portuguese   j) Polish   k) Turkish
l) Greek   m) Italian   n) Swedish

IV. Working with foreign language texts

2. I read the news today (a - c)

a) Mallorca kappt die Kaffeefahrten

Den berüchtigten "Kaffeefahren" auf Mallorca soll es an den Kragen gehen. Bis zu 150 Busse lauern dort täglich auf vorwiegend ältere Urlaubsgäste und
5 schleppen sie zu angeblich spottbilligen Ausflugsfahrten ins Hinterland. In Wirklichkeit geht es bei einem Gratiskaffee dann um beinhartes Geschäft: Profis drehen der eingeschüchterten Kundschaft sündhaft
10 teuere Lamadecken oder Stützstrümpfe an. Jetzt hat der mallorquinische Transportminister Lorenzo Oliver den Schlepperbussen den "Krieg erklärt". Strafbefehle zwischen 4000 und 6000 DM sollen den
15 Kaffeefahrtenneppern Einhalt gebieten. Ab Beginn der Sommersaison hofft der Minister, durch ein neues Regierungsdekret die Fahrten ganz untersagen zu können. Der Anlaß für diese Aktion ist freilich nicht
20 Schamgefühl gegenüber gerupften Gästen, sondern der Neid der örtlichen Hoteliers und Gastronomen: Sie wollen das schnelle Geschäft mit den arglosen Senioren lieber selbst in den Ferienorten machen und
25 hoffen so, den auswärtigen Ramschverkäufern das Handwerk legen zu können. Der Großteil der rund 3000 Anzeigen, die dem Transportministerium schon vorliegen, stammt nämlich von ihnen.

(Schwäbische Zeitung, 27.02.1992)

b) Ladenbesetzer haben Konjunktur

Nach den Hausbesetzern treiben jetzt selbst in den besten Verkaufslagen Londons Ladenbesetzer
5 ihr Unwesen. Die Polizei ist gegen sie weitgehend machtlos. So fand etwa Martin Barnett, Besitzer eines Polstermöbelge-
10 schäfts in der Londoner Edgeware Road, eines Morgens nicht mehr seine Sofas, sondern Damenunterwäsche und billige
15 Videos vor, die laut Werbeplakat am Schaufenster in einem wahnsinnigen Monster-Ausverkauf verhökert werden sollten. In seinen
20 Laden hinein kam Barnett nicht: Die Schlüssel paßten nicht mehr ins Schloß. Die herbeigerufene Polizei konnte nichts ausrichten,
25 denn die Ladenbesetzer wiesen einen Pachtvertrag vor. Daß dieser gefälscht sein muß, hätte Barnett nur in einem teuren und lang-
30 wierigen Prozeß beweisen können. Der Fall Barnett ist der jüngste in einer ganzen Reihe von Ladenbesetzungen. Vor zwei
35 Wochen wurde beispielsweise in der belebten Oxford Street ein Herrenausstatter aus seinem Ladenlokal vertrieben.
40 Auch dort gaben die Besetzer vor, einen Pachtvertrag zu haben. Dasselbe widerfuhr der Firma in mehreren englischen
45 Städten. Wenn ein Ladenbesitzer schließlich eine Räumungsklage erwirkt hat, was bis zu 5000 Pfund kosten kann, sind die Be-
50 setzer auf und davon und haben sich woanders niedergelassen. Inzwischen trauen sich manche Ladenbesitzer schon gar nicht
55 mehr, nachts nach Hause zu gehen.

(Schwäbische Zeitung, 25.09.1991) (epd)

c) Ehemüde Französinnen
Untersuchung des Statistikinstituts

Paris, im September. (afp) Frankreich ist europaweit das Land mit den meisten «Ehen ohne Trauschein» und unehelichen Geburten: 24 Prozent der
5 französischen Kinder kommen außerehelich zur Welt. Dies geht aus einer Untersuchung des staatlichen französischen Statistikinstituts INSEE hervor, die kürzlich in Paris veröffentlicht wurde.
10 Die Zahl der Eheschliessungen in Frankreich ging zwischen 1972 und 1989 fast um die *Hälfte* zurück, und ein Drittel aller Ehen wird wieder geschieden. Die Geburtenfreudigkeit hat darunter jedoch nicht gelitten, denn mit 1,8 Kindern liegt die Französin weiterhin im EG-Durchschnitt. Immer mehr Französinnen sind *berufstätig* und machen derzeit 44 Prozent der aktiven Bevölkerung aus. Das die meisten von ihnen auch nach der Geburt des zweiten Kindes noch weiterarbeiten, ist weitgehend dem fast lückenlosen System der Ganztagsvorschule zu verdanken. Ungetrübt ist das Leben der berufstätigen Französin allerdings nicht; im Durchschnitt ist ihr Gehalt um *ein Drittel* niedriger als das der Männer.

(Neue Züricher Zeitung, 17.09.1992)

2. I read the news today (d - f)

d)

Eine Lektion zum Thema "Alltag in Europa" erteilten die Zollbehörden einem Lehrerehepaar, das sich ausgerechnet auf einer deutsch-französischen Freundschaftsveranstaltung kennengelernt hatte.
Weil der Lehrer aus Kehl regelmäßig in der Straßburger Wohnung seiner französischen Ehefrau übernachtet, sollte er 47 % Mehrwertsteuer für sein neues Auto zahlen. Nachdem der deutsche Fiskus die üblichen 14 Prozent kassiert hatte, griff der Zoll in Straßburg zu und verlangte nochmal 33 %, nach längerer Observierung des Mercedes 300 D, den der deutsche Halter nichtsahnend vor der Wohnung seiner französischen Ehefrau geparkt hatte. Alle Versuche des Bürgers wenigstens nur die deutsche oder die französische Steuer zahlen zu müssen, stießen bei den Verwaltungen beider Länder auf taube Ohren. Denn in der Regel sieht die Praxis so aus: Wer ein Auto nach Frankreich exportiert, löst zwei steuerliche Vorgänge aus. Zum einen fließen 14 % Mehrwertsteuer vom deutschen Fiskus in seine Tasche zurück, zum anderen greift der französische Zoll zu und sorgt dafür, daß 33 % Mehrwertsteuer nach Paris abgeführt werden. Die französischen Behörden fürchten, daß findige Franzosen im Grenzraum dazu übergehen könnnten, Autos mit deutschen Kennzeichen zu fahren. Zugleich mit der Zulassung auf der anderen Seite des Rheins würden dem französischen Staat Steuereinnahmen entgehen. In dieses abschüssige Gelände des deutsch-französischen Mehrwertsteuer-Gefälles ist das Lehrer-Ehepaar offenbar geraten. Erst nach einer Intervention des damaligen Straßburger Oberbürgermeisters und zugleich Präsidenten des Europäischen Parlaments Pierre Pflimlin verzichtete der französische Zoll auf die Besteuerung.

(from *Der Milliarden Joker* by Wogau et al.)

e)

Eine besonders trickreiche "Retourkutsche" gegen das deutsche Importverbot für französisches Bier, das nicht nach den Vorschriften des Reinheitsgebots gebraut ist (das im "Bierurteil" des Europäischen Gerichtshofs vom 12. März 1987 weitgehend aufgehoben wurde), ließ sich die Pariser Regierung im Herbst 1983 einfallen. Opfer des gallischen Einfallsreichtums waren diesmal nicht Video-Rekorder aus Japan, sondern nichtalkoholische Getränke aus Deutschland, deren sprudelnder Export gebremst werden sollte. Die Politik der Nadelstiche schlägt sich in einer Vorschrift nieder, die besagt, daß die in eine Flasche eingedruckte Mengenangabe nicht genügt, sondern daß die auf das Etikett "in mindestens vier Millimeter hohen Buchstaben" aufgedruckt werden muß. Doch damit nicht genug: auf dem Etikett jeder eingeführten Sprudelflasche muß fortan der Name des Importeurs angegeben werden. Daraus ergibt sich die schikanöse Konsequenz, daß die Firmen für jeden ausländischen Handelspartner künftig ein gesondertes Etikett verwenden müssen. Eine Getränkefirma aus dem Schwarzwald wandte sich an den Verfasser, der in der ersten Wahlperiode Generalberichterstatter für den Abbau von Handelshemmnissen war, mit der Bitte um Beistand. Der Export ihrer Produkte aus Peterstal war vorläufig gestoppt worden, nachdem ein Kontrolltrupp der französischen Behörden die nach deutschen Vorschriften etikettierten Flaschen in einem Straßburger Supermarkt aufgespürt hatte. Durch eine Intervention des Verfassers konnten im konkreten Fall wenigstens die bereits produzierten Getränke die Grenze passieren und so der Schaden in Grenzen gehalten werden.

(from *Der Milliarden-Joker* by Wogau et al.)

f)

Ein ausländischer Hersteller von Rasierschaum konnte sein Produkt auf dem deutschen Markt nicht verkaufen, denn er wurde von der deutschen Kosmetikverordnung eingeseift. Die besagte Verordnung schreibt in der Tat vor, daß Seifen, die nicht zur Babypflege taugen, entsprechend kenntlich zu machen sind. Da Rasierschaum eine Seife im Sinne der Verordnung ist, zweifelte ein Ordnungsamt die Verkehrsfähigkeit des Produkts an. So führen bürokratische Seifenblasen den Verbraucherschutz ad absurdum.
In den Genuß des französischen Aperitifs Kir kamen die deutschen Verbraucher nur mit Hilfe des Europäischen Gerichtshofs. Die deutschen Behörden verboten die Einfuhr des Likörs Cassis, weil er den gesetzlich vorgeschriebenen Mindestalkoholgehalt nicht erreichte. In einer richtungsweisenden Entscheidung, auf die später noch einzugehen ist, hat der Gerichtshof entschieden, daß das Einfuhrverbot nicht durch Gründe des Verbraucher- oder Gesundheitsschutzes gerechtfertigt sei, deshalb dürfe das in Frankreich rechtmäßig hergestellte Erzeugnis auch in allen EG-Ländern verkauft werden.

(from *Der Milliarden-Joker* by Wogau et al.)

IV. Working with foreign language texts

3. One out of three

Danish

> Enhver EF-borgers ret til erhvervsudøvelse hvor som helst i Fællesskabet er illusorisk, så lange folk ikke kan andre sprog end deres modersmål.

Portuguese

> O direito de qualquer cidadão europeu ter um emprego em qualquer local do espaço comunitário continuará a ser um logro enquanto esse cidadão não conhecer outras linguas para além da sua lingua materna.

Dutch

> Het recht van iedere Europese burger om waar dan ook in de Gemeenschap zijn beroep uit te oefenen, blijft illusoir zo lang die burger geen andere talen dan zijn moedertaal kent.

(from *Teaching of Foreign Languages* by the Commission of the European Communities)

Fill in the English words.

1	2	3	4	5	6	7	8
9	10	11	12	13	14	15	16
17	18	19	20	21	22	23	24
25	26	27	28	29	30	31	32

✂ —

Solution:

The	right	of	every	European	to	take	up
1	2	3	4	5	6	7	8
an	occupation	anywhere	in	the	Community	will	remain
9	10	11	12	13	14	15	16
an	illusion	until	such	time	as	citizens	have
17	18	19	20	21	22	23	24
knowledge	of	languages	other	than	their	mother	tongue.
25	26	27	28	29	30	31	32

(from *Teaching of Foreign Languages* by the Commission of the European Communities)

C IV. Working with foreign language texts

4. Translation with a difference

Here you have the German and the Dutch version of the same sentence. Try to find the English text by suggesting words to your teacher which you think will appear in the English version. Your teacher will tell you if you are right and where in the text the word appears.

Dutch
> De Gemeenschap zal al haar burgers de magelijkheid bieden zich binnen de Gemeenschap even vrij te verplaatsen als in eigen land.

German
> Jeder Bürger eines Mitgliedstaates wird sich in der Gemeinschaft genauso frei bewegen können wie in seinem eigenen Land.

(from *A Citizen's Europe* by the Office for Official Publications of the European Communities)

Fill in the English words.

1	2	3	4	5	6	7	8
9	10	11	12	13	14	15	16
17	18	19	20	21	22	23	24
25	26						

✂ -

Solution:

To	move	within	the	Community	as	freely	as
1	2	3	4	5	6	7	8
in	one's	own	country	is	a	right	which
9	10	11	12	13	14	15	16
the	Community	is	to	grant	to	each	of
17	18	19	20	21	22	23	24
its	citizens.						
25	26						

(from *A Citizen's Europe* by the Office for Official Publications of the European Communities)

IV. Working with foreign language texts

5. English-French-English

a)

Les religions des Douze

- **FRANCE** : 55,5 millions d'habitants, environ 90 % de catholiques.
  — Musulmans : 3 à 4 millions (l'islam est la deuxième religion de France).
  — Protestants : environ 850 000 (dont 500 000 calvinistes presbytériens et réformés).
  — Juifs : entre 550 000 et 750 000.
  — Orthodoxes : plus de 50 000.
- **RFA** : 61 millions d'habitants.
  — Catholiques : environ 45 % (26,5 millions en 1987).
  — Protestants : 41,1 % (plus de 25 millions, dont 12 millions de luthériens, 13 millions d'unifiés).
  — Juifs : environ 28 000.
  — Musulmans : 2 %.
- **ROYAUME-UNI** : 57 millions d'habitants.
  Eglises établies : Eglise d'Angleterre et d'Ecosse.
  — Anglicans : environ 57 % de la population.
  — Catholiques : 8 % (sur environ 37 millions de chrétiens, 32 millions de protestants).
  — Juifs : plus de 400 000.
  — Musulmans : plus de 1,5 million.
  — Bouddhistes : environ 25 000.
- **IRLANDE** : 3,54 millions d'habitants en 1986. Pas d'Eglise établie.
  — Catholiques : environ 3,4 millions (91 % des catholiques sont pratiquants).
  — Protestants : environ 100 000.
- **PAYS-BAS** : 14,62 millions d'habitants en 1987.
  — Catholiques : 40 %.
  — Protestants : 30 % (Eglise réformée hollandaise : 23 %).
  — Sans religion : 26 %.
- **BELGIQUE** : 9,865 millions d'habitants en 1987.
  — Catholiques : 72 %.
  — Protestants : 24 000.
  — Juifs : 35 000.
- **LUXEMBOURG** : 3 695 00 habitants en 1986.
  — Catholiques : 97 %.
  — Protestants : 1 %.
  — Juifs : 0,2 %.
  — Divers : 1,8 %.
- **ITALIE** : 57,1 millions d'habitants en 1985.
  — Catholiques : plus de 90 %.
  — Protestants : environ 50 000.
- **DANEMARK** : 5,12 millions d'habitants en 1987.
  — Protestants (religion d'Etat) : plus de 91 %.
  — Catholiques : 27 000.
  — Juifs : 8 000.
- **GRÈCE** : 10,03 millions d'habitants en 1987.
  — Orthodoxes (religion officielle) : 97 %.
  — Catholiques : environ 50 000.
  — Musulmans : 1,2 %.
  — Juifs : 5 000 en 1987.
  — Protestants : plus de 5 000.
- **ESPAGNE** : 39 millions d'habitants en 1987.
  — Catholiques : 99 %.
  — Protestants : 40 000.
  — Juifs : environ 12 000.
  — Musulmans : 300 000.
- **PORTUGAL** : 9,74 millions d'habitants en 1986.
  — Catholiques : environ 90 %.
  — Protestants : environ 10 000.
  — Musulmans : environ 15 000.

(from *Le Quotidien de Paris*, 27.10.1989)

b)

F R A N C E

Superficie : 547 026 km². **Population** : 55 millions 500 000 habitants. **Densité** : 101 hab. au km². **Départements outre-mer** : Martinique, Guadeloupe, Guyane, Réunion, St-Pierre-et-Miquelon. **Capitale** : Paris (2 176 200 hab., agglomération : 8 707 000). **Principales grandes villes** : Lyon (413 100, agglomération : 1 220 800), Marseille (874 400, agglomération : 1 110 500), Lille (168 424, agglomération : 936 300), Bordeaux (208 200, agglomération : 640 000), Toulouse (348 000, agglomération : 541 300), Nantes (240 500, agglomération : 464 900). **Langue** : français. **Monnaie** : franc. **Régime** : République. Démocratie parlementaire (deux chambres : l'Assemblée nationale et le Sénat. **Fête nationale** : 14 juillet (prise de la Bastille le 14-7-1789). **Religions** : catholiques, protestants, musulmans, juifs. **PNB par habitant** : 10 900 Ecus. **Principales exportations** : agro-alimentaire (céréales, produits laitiers, œufs, viande, fruits et légumes, produits de l'industrie alimentaire), matériel de transport (automobile, ferroviaire), chimie, biens d'équipements, métallurgie.

c)

E S P A G N E

Superficie : 504 782 km². **Population** : 39 millions d'habitants. **Densité** : 77 hab. au km². **Outre-mer** : Canaries. **Capitale** : Madrid (3 188 300 hab.). **Principales grandes villes** : Barcelone (1 754 900 hab.), Valence (751 700), Séville (653 800), Saragosse (590 750), Malaga (503 200), Bilbao (433 000). **Langues** : espagnol ou castillan (langue officielle nationale), basque, catalan, galicien, valencien (langues officielles régionales). **Monnaie** : peseta. **Régime** : monarchie parlementaire. Deux chambres : le Congrès des députés, et le Sénat. Nationalités et régions ont droit à l'autonomie. **Fête nationale** : 24 juin (Saint-Jean, fête du roi). **Religions** : catholiques (99 %), protestants, juifs, musulmans. **PNB par habitant** : 4 860 Ecus. **Principales exportations** : agro-alimentaire (oranges, poisson, vin), métallurgie, textile, chaussures, articles manufacturés (pneus, ciment, jouets).

d)

P O R T U G A L

Superficie : 92 100 km². **Population** : 10 millions 300 000 habitants. **Densité** : 112 hab. au km². **Outre-mer** : Açores, Madère. **Capitale** : Lisbonne (817 700 hab.). **Principales grandes villes** : Porto (330 200 hab.), Amadora (93 700), Setubal (76 800), Coimbra (71 800). **Langue** : portugais. **Monnaie** : escudo. **Régime** : république. Démocratie parlementaire. **Fêtes nationales** : 10 juin (jour de Camoes, dep. 1910), 5 octobre (proclamation de la République), 1er décembre (indépendance recouvrée), 25 avril (jour de la liberté, anniversaire de la Révolution des Œillets en 1974). **Religion** : catholiques (90 %). **PNB par habitant** : 2 340 Ecus. **Principales exportations** : textile (habillement), agro-alimentaire (vin, bois, pâte à papier), industrie des métaux (matériel électrique, fer et acier), articles manufacturés (articles en liège, papier-carton).

(from *PHOSPHORE*, 1989)

IV. Working with foreign language texts **C**

5. English - French - English

Worksheet

From the material provided, try to find out whether the following statements are true:

	True	False

1. Most EC citizens are Catholics.
2. There are more Jews in Belgium than in Spain.
3. The UK has the largest Muslim population of all EC countries.
4. There are more Catholics in Spain than there are in Italy.
5. There are more Catholics than Protestants in Germany.
6. There are more Protestants in Ireland than in Belgium.
7. There are more Jews in Europe than Muslims.
8. Spain is bigger than France.
9. Barcelona has more inhabitants than Lisbon.
10. Population density in Portugal is lower than in France.
11. Portugal has more national holidays than Spain and France put together.

✂ —

Solution:
True: 1, 2, 3, 5 (figures before reunification), 6, 9, 11
False: 4, 7, 8, 10

✂ —

Variation

Use the French texts (a - l) given on page 76 and try to answer the following questions:

1. Which country is the biggest?
2. Which country is the smallest?
3. How many languages are spoken in the 12 countries?
4. In which European country are the most languages spoken?
5. Which country is most densely populated?
6. Which country is least densely populated?
7. Which countries are republics?
8. Which countries are monarchies?
9. Which countries are the oldest members of the EC?
10. Which countries became members of the EC latest?

IV. Working with foreign language texts

5. English - French - English

a) DANEMARK

Superficie : 43070 km². **Population** : 5 millions 120000 habitants. Densité : 118,9 hab. au km². **Capitale** : Copenhague (418600 hab., agglomération : 1722800). **Principales grandes villes** : Aarhus (252000 hab.), Odense (171400), Aalborg (154750), Esbjerg (80500), Randers (61100). **Langue** : danois. **Monnaie** : couronne danoise. **Régime** : monarchie parlementaire. Parlement : Folketing (179 membres). **Fête nationale** : 5 juin (Constitution de 1849). **Religions** : luthériens (97 %), catholiques, baptistes, méthodistes, israélites. **PNB par habitant** : 9200 Ecus. **Principales exportations** : agro-alimentaire (viande, produits laitiers, poisson), industrie des métaux (équipements frigorifiques, matériel électrique), construction navale, articles manufacturés (meubles), énergie (pétrole de la mer du Nord).

b) FRANCE

Superficie : 547026 km². **Population** : 55 millions 500000 habitants. Densité : 101 hab. au km². **Départements outre-mer** : Martinique, Guadeloupe, Guyane, Réunion, St-Pierre-et-Miquelon. **Capitale** : Paris (2176200 hab., agglomération : 8707000). **Principales grandes villes** : Lyon (413100, agglomération : 1220800), Marseille (874400, agglomération : 1110500), Lille (168424, agglomération : 936300), Bordeaux (208200, agglomération : 640000), Toulouse (348000, agglomération : 541300), Nantes (240500, agglomération : 464900). **Langue** : français. **Monnaie** : franc. **Régime** : République. Démocratie parlementaire (deux chambres : l'Assemblée nationale et le Sénat). **Fête nationale** : 14 juillet (prise de la Bastille le 14-7-1789). **Religions** : catholiques, protestants, musulmans, juifs. **PNB par habitant** : 10900 Ecus. **Principales exportations** : agro-alimentaire (céréales, produits laitiers, œufs, viande, fruits et légumes, produits de l'industrie alimentaire), matériel de tranport (automobile, ferroviaire), chimie, biens d'équipements, métallurgie.

c) ALLEMAGNE FÉDÉRALE

Superficie : 249147 km², y compris Berlin-Ouest. **Population** : 61 millions d'habitants. Densité : 246 hab. au km². **Capitale** : Bonn. **Principales grandes villes** : Berlin-Ouest (1860500 hab.), Hambourg (1617800), Munich (1284300), Cologne (953300), Essen (635200), Francfort (614700). **Langue** : allemand. **Monnaie** : mark. **Régime** : république fédérale. Démocratie parlementaire : deux assemblées, le Bundesrat et le Bundestag. C'est le Bundestag (520 députés) qui élit le chancelier. **Fête nationale** : 17 juin, journée de l'unité allemande (commémoration des émeutes du 17-6-1953 à Berlin-Est). **Religions** : protestants (41%), catholiques (44,6%), musulmans (2%), juifs. **PNB par habitants** : 12330 Ecus. **Principales exportations** : chimie (caoutchouc, engrais, textile synthétique, matières plastiques, produits pharmaceutiques), automobile, métallurgie, équipements électriques et électroniques, télécommunications et téléphonie, industrie alimentaire (bière).

d) GRÈCE

Superficie : 131944 km². **Population** : 10 millions d'habitants. Densité : 75,7 hab. au km². **Capitale** : Athènes (885800 hab.). **Principales grandes villes** : Thessalonique (706180 hab.), Patras (154600), Héraklion (111000), Volos (107400), Larissa (102250). **Langue** : grec. **Monnaie** : drachme. **Fêtes nationales** : 25 mars (soulèvement de 1821 contre les Turcs), 28 octobre (invasion italienne de 1940 repoussée). **Régime** : république. Démocratie parlementaire. **Religions** : orthodoxes (97 %), musulmans (1,2 %), chrétiens divers (0,8 %). **PNB par habitant** : 3260 Ecus. **Principales exportations** : agro-alimentaire (fruits, tabac), produits miniers (produits pétroliers), industrie des métaux (fer et acier, aluminium), textile (bonneterie), produits manufacturés (ciment).

e) IRLANDE

Superficie : 70280 km². **Population** : 3 millions 580000 habitants. Densité : 50,9 hab. au km². **Capitale** : Dublin (502300 hab.). **Principales grandes villes** : Cork (133200 hab.), Limerick (56200), Dun Laoghaire (54500). **Langues** : anglais, irlandais. **Monnaie** : livre irlandaise. **Régime** : république parlementaire (deux assemblées : la Chambre des députés, et le Sénat). **Fête nationale** : 17 mars (Saint-Patrick). **Religions** : catholiques (91 %), Église d'Irlande, presbytériens, méthodistes. **PNB par habitant** : 5840 Ecus. **Principales exportations** : agro-alimentaire (bovins, produits laitiers), chimie, industrie des métaux (matériel électrique), textile (vêtements).

f) GRANDE-BRETAGNE

Superficie : 244046 km². **Population** : 56 millions 600000 habitants. Densité : 232 hab. au km². **Capitale** : Londres (6756000 hab.). **Principales grandes villes** : Birmingham (1012900 hab.), Leeds (714000), Sheffield (542700), Liverpool (502500), Bradford (463900), Manchester (457500), Edimbourg (440900). **Langues** : anglais (langue officielle), gallois. **Monnaie** : livre sterling (pound). **Régime** : monarchie constitutionnelle, démocratie parlementaire (deux assemblées : la Chambre des Communes et la Chambre des Lords). **Religions** : anglicans, chrétiens (protestants, catholiques romains). **PNB par habitant** : 8050 Ecus. **Principales exportations** : industrie des métaux (équipements industriels, matériel électrique, moteurs), chimie, automobile, énergie (pétrole, gaz naturel), agro-alimentaire (whisky, orge, ovins), articles manufacturés (instruments d'analyse et de contrôle).

g) ITALIE

Superficie : 301225 km². **Population** : 57 millions 300000 habitants. Densité : 190 hab. au km². **Capitale** : Rome (2834000 hab.). **Principales grandes villes** : Milan (1580800 hab.), Naples (1209000), Turin (1093400), Gênes (754400), Palerme (707700), Bologne (454700). **Langues** : italien (langue officielle), allemand, français, slovène, ladin, occitan, sarde, frioulan. **Monnaie** : lire. **Régime** : république. Démocratie parlementaire (deux assemblées : la Chambre des députés et le Sénat). **Fêtes nationales** : 25 avril (libération), 2 juin (fondation de la République), 4 novembre (victimes de 1916). **Religions** : catholiques romains (99,6 %). **PNB par habitant** : 7330 Ecus. **Principales exportations** : industrie des métaux (matériel électrique, équipements industriels), automobile, textile, chimie (plastique), produits pétroliers raffinés, agro-alimentaire (fruits, vin), articles manufacturés (meubles, bijoux).

h) PORTUGAL

Superficie : 92100 km². **Population** : 10 millions 300000 habitants. Densité : 112 hab. au km². **Outre-mer** : Açores, Madère. **Capitale** : Lisbonne (817700 hab.). **Principales grandes villes** : Porto (330200 hab.), Amadora (93700), Setubal (76800), Coimbra (71800). **Langue** : portugais. **Monnaie** : escudo. **Régime** : république. Démocratie parlementaire. **Fêtes nationales** : 10 juin (jour de Camoes, dep. 1910), 5 octobre (proclamation de la République), 1er décembre (indépendance recouvrée), 25 avril (jour de la liberté, anniversaire de la Révolution des Œillets en 1974). **Religion** : catholiques (90 %). **PNB par habitant** : 2340 Ecus. **Principales exportations** : textile (habillement), agro-alimentaire (vin, bois, pâte à papier), industrie des métaux (matériel électrique, fer et acier), articles manufacturés (articles en liège, papier-carton).

i) PAYS-BAS

Superficie : 40844 km². **Population** : 14 millions 560000 habitants. Densité : 356 hab. au km². **Capitale** : La Haye (674600 hab.). **Principales grandes villes** : Amsterdam (1006900 hab.), Rotterdam (1025600), Utrecht (511200), Eindhoven (376200), Arnhem (294100). **Langue** : néerlandais. **Monnaie** : florin. **Régime** : monarchie constitutionnelle. Démocratie parlementaire. **Fête nationale** : 30 avril (jour de la reine). **Religions** : catholiques (36 %), protestants (26 %), sans religion (35 %). **PNB par habitant** : 9790 Ecus. **Principales exportations** : agro-alimentaire (bovins, porcins, légumes, bulbes et fleurs), énergie (gaz naturel, gazole, fuel, carburants), chimie, industrie des métaux (fer et acier, matériel électrique, équipements industriels, télécommunications), articles manufacturés divers (papier-carton, appareils photo).

j) BELGIQUE

Superfie : 30519 km². **Population** : 9 millions 850000 habitants. Densité : 325 hab. au km². **Capitale** : Bruxelles (976500 hab.). **Principales grandes villes** : Anvers (927200 hab.), Liège (618500), Gand (484900), Charleroi (450100), Malines (291400), Ostende (270900), Bruges (252400). **Langues** : français, flamand, allemand. **Monnaie** : franc belge. **Régime** : monarchie constitutionnelle parlementaire (deux chambres : le Sénat, et la Chambre des représentants). **Fête nationale** : 21 juillet (prestation du serment constitutionnel de Léopold Ier en 1831). **Religions** : catholiques (72 %), protestants, israélites, anglicans. **PNB par habitant** : 9330 Ecus. **Principales exportations** : métallurgie, chimie, automobile, produits pétroliers raffinés, agro-alimentaire (viande), diamants taillés, produits manufacturés (tapis, confection, films et papier-photo).

k) LUXEMBOURG

Superficie : 2586 km². **Population** : 370000 habitants. Densité : 143 hab. au km². **Capitale** : Luxembourg (79000 hab.). **Principales grandes villes** : Esch-sur-Alzette (25100 hab.), Dudelange (14100), Differdange (8600). **Langues** : français, allemand, dialecte, luxembourgeois. **Monnaies** : franc luxembourgeois, franc belge. **Régime** : monarchie constitutionnelle (Grand-Duc). **Fête nationale** : 23 juin (anniversaire du chef d'État, célébration officielle). **Religions** : catholiques (97 %), protestants, juifs. **PNB par habitant** : 11480 Ecus. **Principales exportations** : métaux, caoutchouc, plastiques, agro-alimentaire (bovins, lait), textile.

l) ESPAGNE

Superficie : 504782 km². **Population** : 39 millions d'habitants. Densité : 77 hab. au km². **Outre-mer** : Canaries. **Capitale** : Madrid (3188300 hab.). **Principales grandes villes** : Barcelone (1754900 hab.), Valence (751700), Séville (653800), Saragosse (590750), Malaga (503200), Bilbao (433000). **Langues** : espagnol ou castillan (langue officielle nationale), basque, catalan, galicien, valencien (langues officielles régionales). **Monnaie** : peseta. **Régime** : monarchie parlementaire. Deux chambres : le Congrès des députés, et le Sénat. Nationalités et régions ont droit à l'autonomie. **Fête nationale** : 24 juin (Saint-Jean, fête du roi). **Religions** : catholiques (99 %), protestants, juifs, musulmans. **PNB par habitant** : 4860 Ecus. **Principales exportations** : agro-alimentaire (oranges, poisson, vin), métallurgie, textile, chaussures, articles manufacturés (pneus, ciment, jouets).

(from *PHOSPHORE*, 1989)

V. Facts, texts and figures

1. Europe by numbers

1. In Germany, _____ adults are functionally illiterate.

2. There are around _____ Chinese take-aways in Britain.

3. Number of golfers in England: _____

4. Number of registered cricketers in the Netherlands: _____

5. One in every _____ citizens in the Community is over 60.

6. In England and Wales _____ marriages per 1,000 will end in divorce.

7. Of the 600,000 people currently practising medicine in the Community, only _____ work outside the country in which they obtained their qualification.

8. Around the Mediterranean coast are _____ cities with populations of 10,000 or more.

9. Mr. Delors earns $_____ a year.

10. Denmark now has _____ television sets for every 1,000 people.

Solutions:
1) three million   2) 7,000   3) 644,000
4) 5,000   5) five   6) 12.8
7) 2,000   8) 537   9) 217,000   10) 386

----

2. The word rose

Text to go with the activity on page 33.

Custom-built Franglais sought by Kent police

John Carvel

KENT police want to develop a specialised version of Franglais for communicating with their French counterparts when the Channel Tunnel opens in 1993.

A £100,000 research contract sponsored by British Telecom will go to a university linguistics department to produce a new language in "Copperanto" to eliminate confusion.

Mr. Ted Crew, deputy chief constable of Kent, said yesterday that police were being taught to speak French, but there was a danger of misunderstandings when shades of meaning were called for.

The two forces will have joint responsibility for the tunnel.

Mr. Crew envisaged a language which might involve the creation of new words and could be used on computers and the telephone, he told journalists at Association of Chief Police Officers' conference in Cardiff.

The French are being kept informed but have not yet signed up for any joint venture in further corrupting their language.

(The Guardian, 15.06.1989)

V. Facts, texts and figures

2. The word rose

Here's another set of words from a different text (see below).

```
                    door bell
        teeth                       souvenir
   Dutch woman                           lie
       carving knife            washing up
            spinach              ring
                      caller
```

✂ -

OLIVER PRITCHETT
Small change for hands that do dishes

ONE of the worst consequences of closer EC integration is that all those tiresome surveys about our various domestic habits have become Europe-wide. We can now compare what percentage of British males clean their shoes less than once a fortnight with what proportion of Italian women brush their teeth three times a day. This can be a real conversation-stopper in your local bistro or Bierkeller.

The latest survey, the result of an EC "Eurobarometer" poll, concerns the domestic chores undertaken by family men. Greek, Italian, Portuguese and West German men are enthusiastic shoppers, while the British male emerges as the champion when it comes to washing-up. As many, as seven out of 10 men in Britain said they took no principal responsibility for shopping, cleaning, cooking, dressing the children or taking them to school.

I believe I can remember the occasion when this survey was conducted. I was washing up at the time. Not alone. My wife was drying.

This I admit, was another instance of male chauvinism. Power resides with the person with their arms in the sink; they set the pace. The washer decides if little plates come before glasses and spoons take precedence over forks. The drier-up can only wait for the next object to be put on the draining board. The washer-up can exasperate the drier-up by holding up the procedure with the officious scouring of a pan.

"Why are you always the one who washes?" my wife asked, looking enviously at the rich lather that was being so kind to my hands.

"Actually, I am the one who washes in 72 per cent of kitchen sink scenarios. I am sure this is much less than say, a Spaniard. And if your were washing-up with a Frenchman you would hardly ever get a look in with the Brillo pad.

My wife pointed out that I had left a trace of mustard on the side of a plate and a shred of spinach on the colander. I was upset. British men are 30 per cent more likely to be offended by criticism of their washing-up than men from the Irish Republic. And I told my wife that when she mentioned the mustard she was lucky I was not Belgian.

Our discussion was interrupted by a ring at the door bell. As 88 per cent of all rings at British door bells are answered by men, I went to the door. There was a woman standing there, holding a clipboard. As she was Dutch, I guessed that she must be conducting a survey. More Dutch women go into market research than women from any other EC country. Their nearest challengers are German women, but this woman was almost certainly not German. The clogs were the clue. Less than one per cent of German women wear clogs. I read that interesting statistic on a souvenir drying-up cloth.

The Dutch woman followed me into the kitchen and explained that she was doing this survey on household chores. We said we would answer her questions while we finished the washing-up.

"I'll put away", the Dutch woman offered. "Thank goodness you are not Portuguese. The Portuguese are much stickier about answering questionnaires."

She asked us who did the bed-making and we said it was about 50-50. She asked where the fish slice went and we said it went in the second drawer next to the carving knife. "How very Danish," she commented.

She asked who did most of the shopping and we had an argument about that. She pointed out the bit of mustard on the side of the plate and I was four per cent more offended than I had been the first time. She inquired about who did the most vacuuming and my wife said it was odd that Dutch women never seemed to know where to put the frying-pan when it was washed up. Our caller was six per cent more offended by this than I had been about the mustard.

After this, the conversation got quite animated. I was so distracted that I took her clipboard and gave it a good scrub. She was horrified. "What about all my decor?" she cried. "You have wiped it all away. What shall I do?"

"Make it up," I said. "I can't answer any more questions; I've got all the ironing to do." This was a lie.

(The Telegraph, 12.07.1992)

V. Facts, texts and figures   **C**

3. Scrambled texts

a) Scrambled text

   Kent could be swamped by 40-
the Channel tunnel if proper pro-
1,500 lorries a day off Kent's
freight trains daily to the tunnel
5 roads, by operating some 30
British Architects says.
British rail's plans for tunnel
vision for freight movements is
roads will not be replaced by an-
10 freight envisage taking more than
when it opens in 1993.
said: "If the tunnel is a success
there can be no guarantee that
But in an interim report, James
15 not made, the Royal Institute of
Elkerton, director of RIBA's
Channel tunnel research unit,
ton lorries after the opening of
the 1,500 lorries taken off the
20 other 1,500 or more."

Original text (see scrambled text a)

   Kent could be swamped by 40-
ton lorries after the opening of
the Channel tunnel if proper pro-
vision for freight movements is
5 not made, the Royal Institute of
British Architects says.
British rail's plans for tunnel
freight envisage taking more than
1,500 lorries a day off Kent's
10 roads, by operating some 30
freight trains daily to the tunnel
when it opens in 1993.
But in an interim report, James
Elkerton, director of REBA's
15 Channel tunnel research unit,
said: " If the tunnel is a success
there can be no guarantee that
the 1,500 lorries taken off the
roads will not be replaced by
20 another 1,500 or more."

(The Independent, 04.04.1989)

b) Scrambled text

   The French do it. The Ital-
boosting business by putting
British get embarrassed when.
But because the British sel-
5 cans do it best of all.
have seized on the chance of
ians do it. And the Ameri-
It's symptomatic of what
dom complain, two companies
10 Other nations might call it
Research has shown that the
some psychologists call 'the
stiff upper lip syndrome'.
the test.
15 they complain in public.
this peculiar British trait to
'stupidity'.

Original text (see scrambled text b)

   The French do it. The Italians do it. And the Ameri-
cans do it best of all.
But because the British sel-
5 dom complain, two companies
have seized on the chance of
boosting business by putting
this peculiar British trait to
the test.
10 Research has shown that the
British get embarrassed when
they complain in public.
It´s symptomatic of what
some psychologists call 'the
15 stiff upper lip syndrome'.
Other nations might call it
'stupidity'.

(Daily Mail, 09.03.1989)

VI. A mixed bag

3. Find a European

Name(s)	Find a European who...
	1. can say *Guten Tag* in more than two EC languages
	2. has been to more than three EC countries
	3. has been to the cinema in more than two EC countries
	4. can name a Portuguese artist
	5. knows the name of the President of Italy
	6. has hitch-hiked in an EC country other than Germany
	7. prefers American English to British English
	8. knows the names of at least four minority languages in the EC
	9. speaks Esperanto
	10. did not vote in the last EP election
	11. has eaten fish and chips in Britain and pizza in Italy
	12. has had a traffic accident in an EC country other than Germany
	13. has bought newspapers in more than two EC countries
	14. has had to go to an EC capital on business
	15. knows the name of the president of the European Parliament
	16. has been to the cinema in more than two EC capitals
	17. knows the names of the three biggest cities in Britain
	18. had travelled to East Germany before the Berlin Wall fell
	19. can name all nine official EC languages
	20. prefers British beer to German beer

VI. A mixed bag   C

4. Rain in Spain?

Around the world (Yesterday's lunchtime reports)

		C	F			C	F			C	F
Ajaccio	S	27	81	Geneva	S	27	81	Peking	C	28	82
Algiers	S	39	102	Gibraltar	S	30	86	Perth	S	17	63
Amsterdam	S	26	79	Glasgow	C	17	63	Prague	S	29	84
Athens	F	28	82	Helsinki	F	21	70	Reykjavik	F	14	57
Bahrain	F	34	93	Innsbruck	S	30	86	Rhodes	S	27	81
Barcelona	S	26	79	Inverness	F	18	64	Rlyadh	S	42	108
Beirut	F	27	81	Istanbul	F	23	73	Rome	S	29	84
Belgrade	S	26	79	Jersey	S	25	77	Salzburg	S	29	84
Berlin	S	31	88	Jo'burg	S	19	66	Seoul	F	28	82
❖Bermuda	S	30	86	Karachi	F	30	86	Singapore	F	28	82
Biarritz	F	24	75	Larnaca	S	29	84	Stockholm	C	21	70
Birmingham	R	16	61	Las Palmas	S	24	75	Strasbourg	S	30	86
Bombay	R	28	82	Lisbon	C	24	75	Sydney	R	10	50
Bordeaux	S	33	91	Locarno	C	27	81	Tangier	S	26	79
❖Boston	F	23	73	London	C	23	73	Tel Aviv	C	28	82
Bristol	R	16	61	❖Los Angeles	S	25	77	Tenerife	S	29	84
Brussels	S	27	81	Luxembourg	S	29	84	Tokyo	S	32	90
Budapest	S	27	81	Madrid	S	34	93	Tunis	S	32	90
❖B Aires	F	11	52	Majorca	S	34	93	Valencia	S	32	90
Cairo	S	32	90	Malaga	S	33	91	❖Vancouver	S	23	73
Cape Town	S	16	61	Malta	S	27	81	Venice	S	28	82
Cardiff	R	15	59	Manchester	R	18	64	Vienna	S	27	81
Casablanca	F	24	75	Melbourne	F	11	52	Warsaw	S	26	79
❖Chicago	F	28	82	❖Miami	F	31	88	❖Washington	F	32	90
Cologne	S	29	84	❖Montreal	F	23	73	Wellington	F	11	52
Copenhagen	F	23	73	Moscow	R	18	64	Zurich	S	29	84
Corfu	S	32	90	Munich	S	29	84				
❖Dallas	F	31	88	Nairobi	F	25	77	C, cloudy; Dr, drizzle; F, fair; Fg,			
❖Denver	F	28	82	Naples	S	31	88	fog; H, hail; R, rain; SL, sleet;			
Dublin	F	18	64	❖Nassau	C	31	88	Sn, snow; S, sunny; Th, thunder.			
Edinburgh	F	20	68	Newcastle	F	21	70	❖ (Previous day's readings)			
Faro	S	33	91	❖New York	S	31	88				
Florence	S	31	88	Nice	S	28	82				
Frankfurt	S	31	88	Oporto	F	20	68				
Funchal	S	25	77	Oslo	F	23	73	(The Guardian, 1992)			
				Paris	S	31	88				

VI. A mixed bag

11. European treasure chest

12. A language learning loop

On learning languages

Most people agree that a knowledge of foreign languages is more important than ever in the context of a united Europe. Not only will you have to know what CAP stands for, or what ECU means (and how much it is worth), what is meant by MEP or VAT, you will also have to be fluent in the use of at least one official EC other than your own. But how does one go about learning languages?

As a language learner your should be inquisitive. Time and again you will have to tackle unknown words and phrases. Asking questions about the things you have not understood shows that you are a sophisticated language learner because nobody - not even your teacher - can know all the words that exist in the target language.

Some people find asking questions embarrassing. They fear that the teacher or the other students might think that they are 'thick' if they have to admit to their ignorance. Quite the opposite! Only if you keep asking questions will you later be able to use the language deftly. If you <u>don't</u> ask, you'll soon be in a quandary.

One of the most important things to ask questions about is idioms because these can't be translated literally. If someone talks to you like a *Dutch uncle*, if someone suggests to you to *go Dutch*, if someone has got a lot of *Dutch courage*, it doesn't help you very much to know that Dutch is a language spoken in the Netherlands. A literal translation just doesn't work.

Of course you need to know how to ask questions. So here are some examples:

❖ Does *germane* mean the same as *German*?

❖ What's the meaning of *inquisitiveness*?

❖ Could you please explain the difference between a *French window* and an ordinary one?

❖ What would be the opposite of *thick* as used in this text?

❖ Which is correct: the *Spaniards* or the *Spanish*?

❖ What's *to tackle* in German?

❖ What does *VAT* stand for?

❖ How do you say *anspruchsvoll* in English?

❖ What's the German word for *quandary*?

❖ What's the exact meaning of *deftly*?

❖ How does one translate *Europäerin* into English?

❖ Is there a German idiom for *It's all Greek to me*?

The above text could serve as a lead-in into a discussion of what makes a *good* language learner.

VI. A mixed bag

14. Shopping for Europe

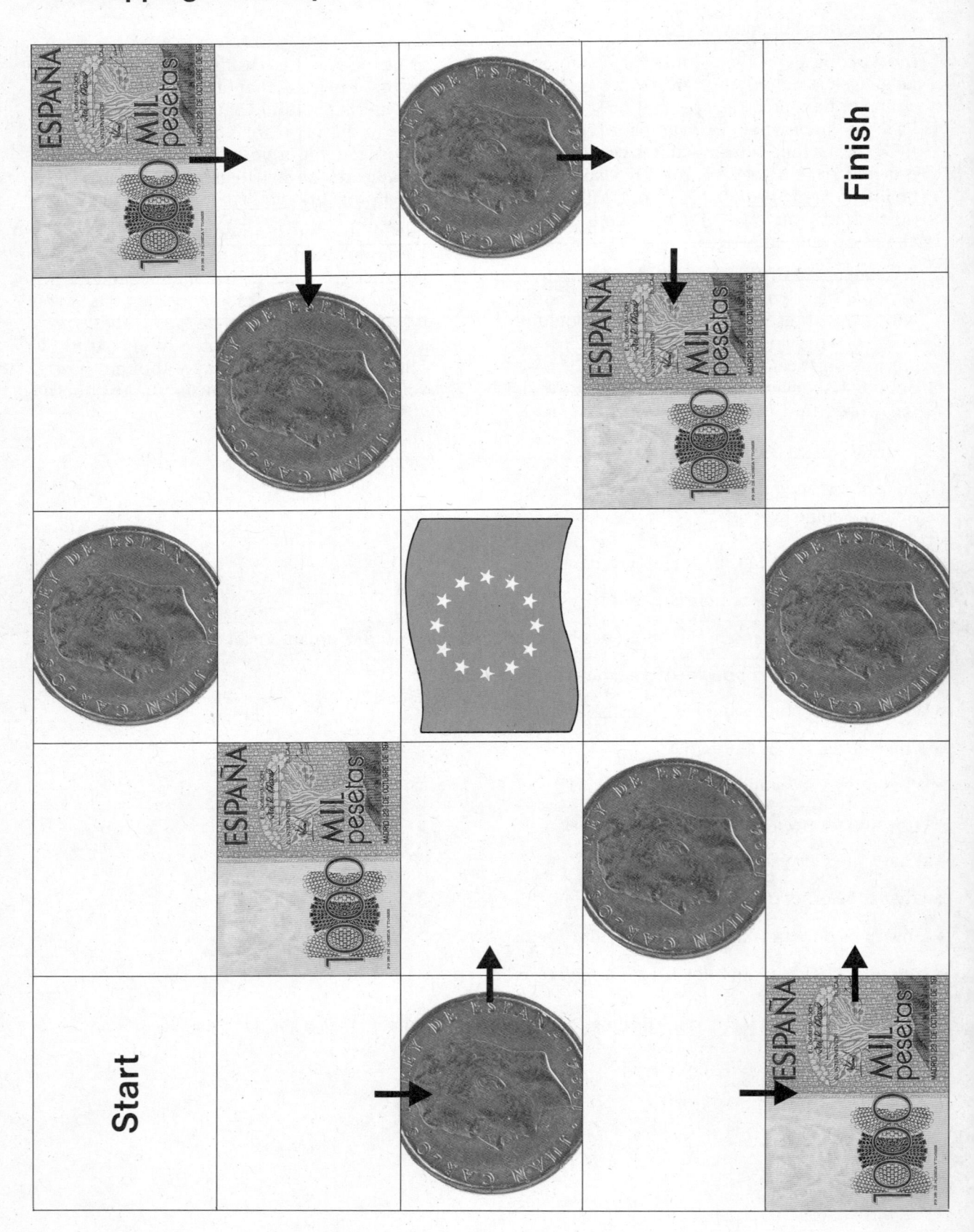

VI. A mixed bag

15. My Place - the Video

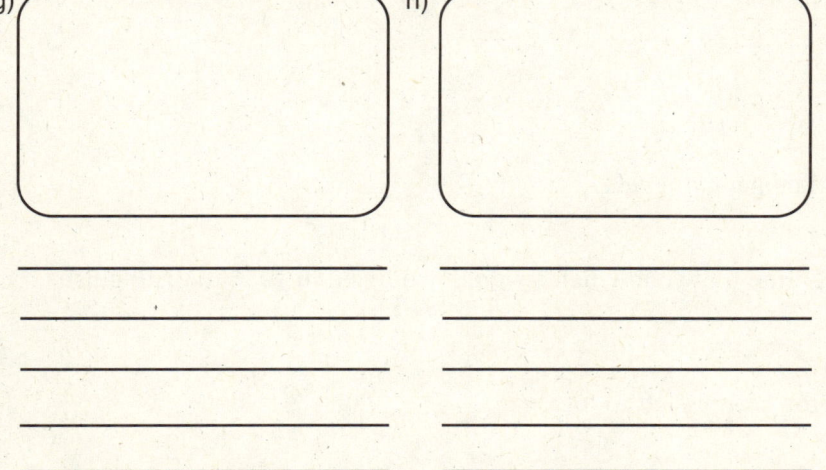

a)

b)

c)

d)

e)

f)

g)

h)

VI. A mixed bag

23. Choose your own topic

Discuss the following sentences with your partner.

1. Spain has one of the highest rates of babies abandoned in Europe, averaging two every day.

2. Keep Britain tidy - kill a tourist.

3. More than 500 refugees are applying for political asylum in Germany every day.

4. Just because you are paranoid doesn't mean they're not out to get you.

5. Queen Beatrix of the Netherlands, 53, is to use an energy-saving bus to take visiting dignitaries around the country.

6. Don't put all your eggs in one basket.

7. Corsica's population, 85 per cent ethnically Corsican in 1952, is now only 50 per cent Corsican. Everywhere you see the graffiti: 'I francesi fora!' - 'Out with the French!'

8. French people are drinking about half as much alcohol as they did a generation ago - but they still top Europe's league of drinkers.

9. Is there a man among you will offer his son a stone when he asks for bread, or a snake when he asks for fish?

10. The British Museum was the most popular London spot for tourists in 1990, according to English Tourist Board figures. Almost five million people visited the museum last year. The most popular site which charges admission was Madame Tussaud's Waxworks, which had 2,54 million visitors in the same period.

11. Let sleeping dogs lie.

12. The more you drive the less intelligent you get.

13. Most French people have forgotten that yellow lights were introduced in 1936 to distinguish French vehicles from German.

14. Freedom's just another word for nothing left to lose.

Make your own EUROtic material

1. Outline map of the European Community (EC) member states

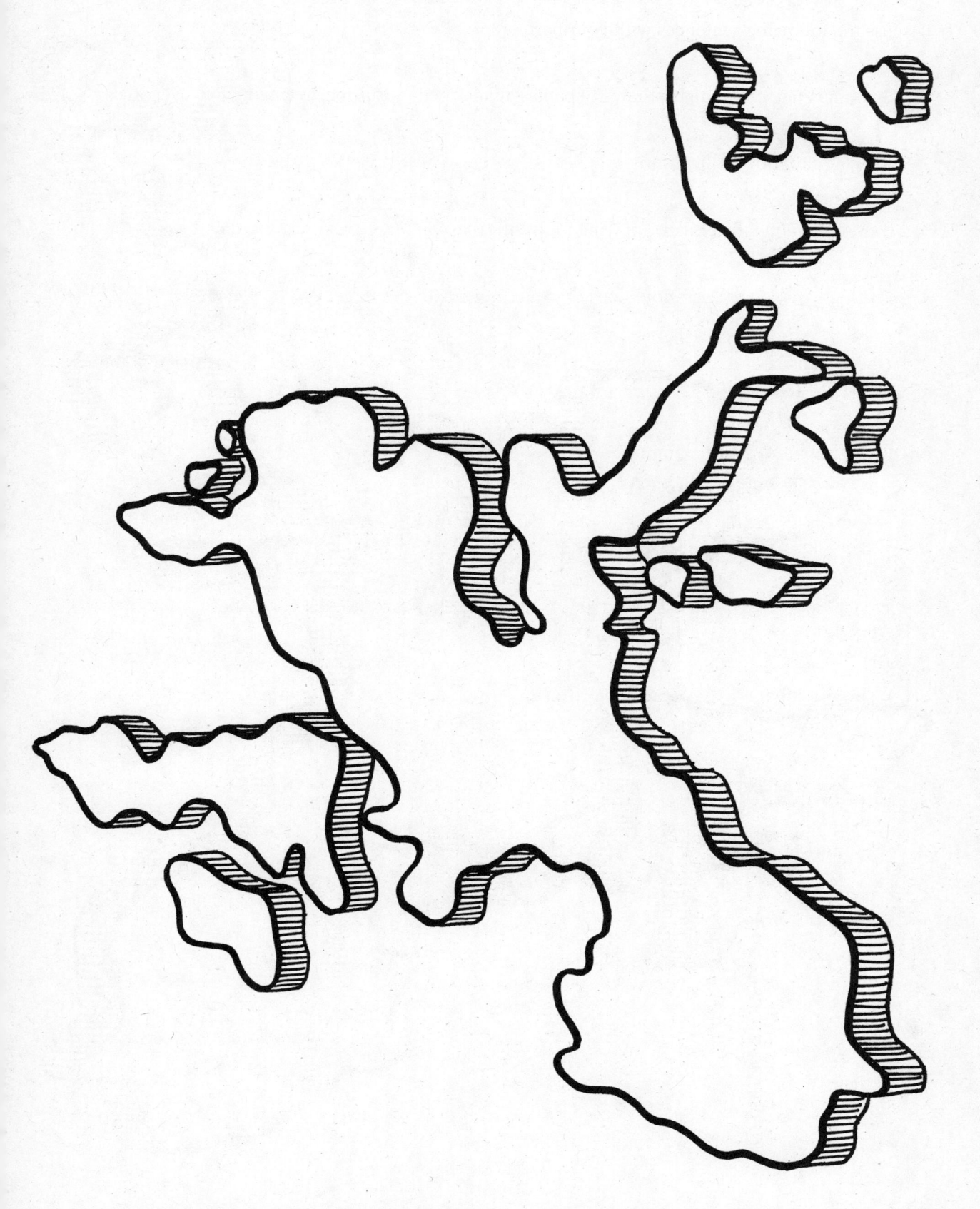

C *Make your own EUROtic material*

2. Map of the EC with names of states and capitals

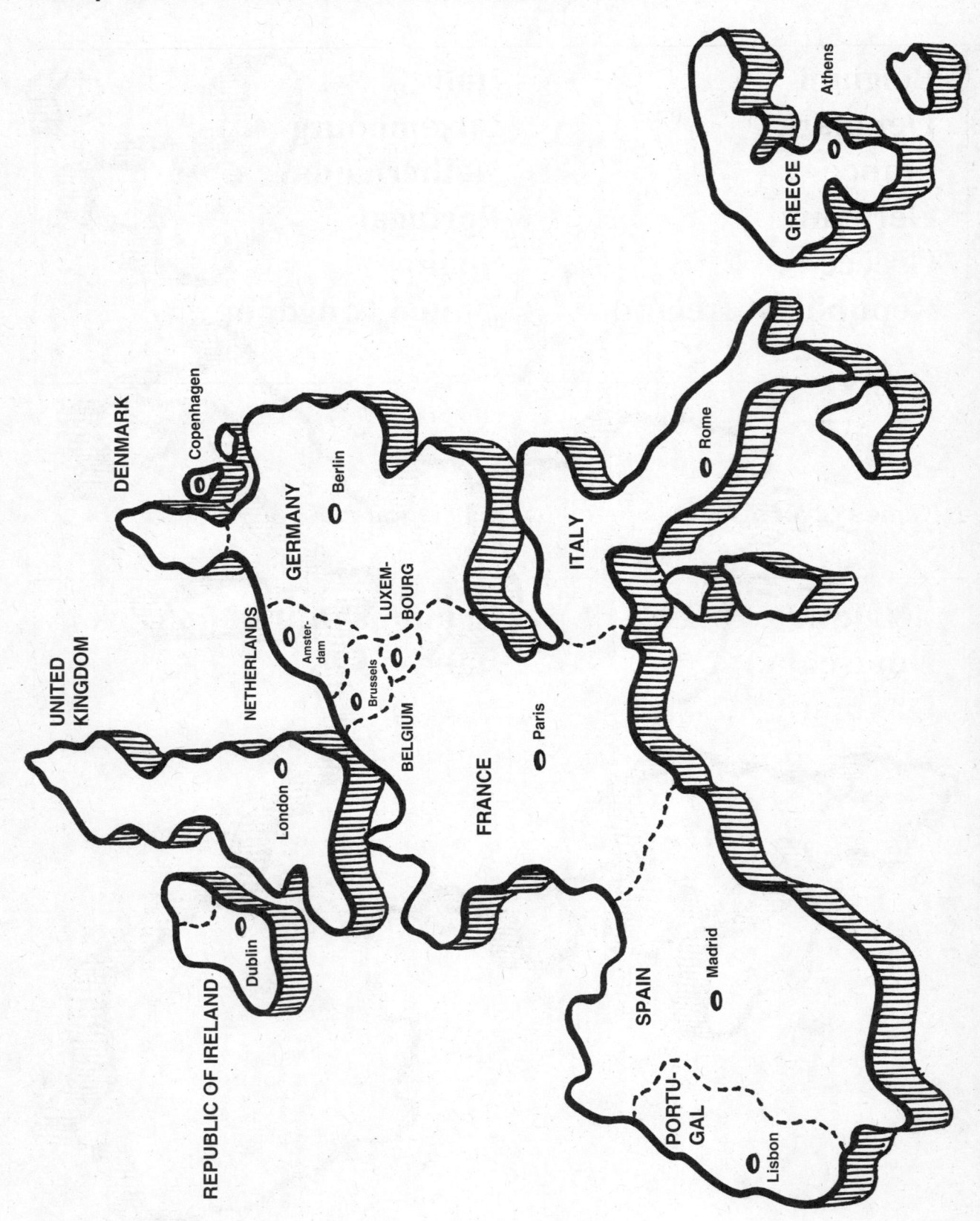

Make your own EUROtic material C

3. Names of all EC states in English

Belgium	**Italy**
Denmark	**Luxembourg**
France	**Netherlands**
Germany	**Portugal**
Greece	**Spain**
Republic of Ireland	**United Kingdom**

✂ ---

4. Names of all EC states in the national languages

Belgique / België	**Republic of Ireland (Eire)**
Deutschland	**Italia**
Danmark	**Luxembourg**
Ellas	**Nederland**
España	**Portugal**
France	**United Kingdom**

Make your own EUROtic material

5. Flags of all the EC states

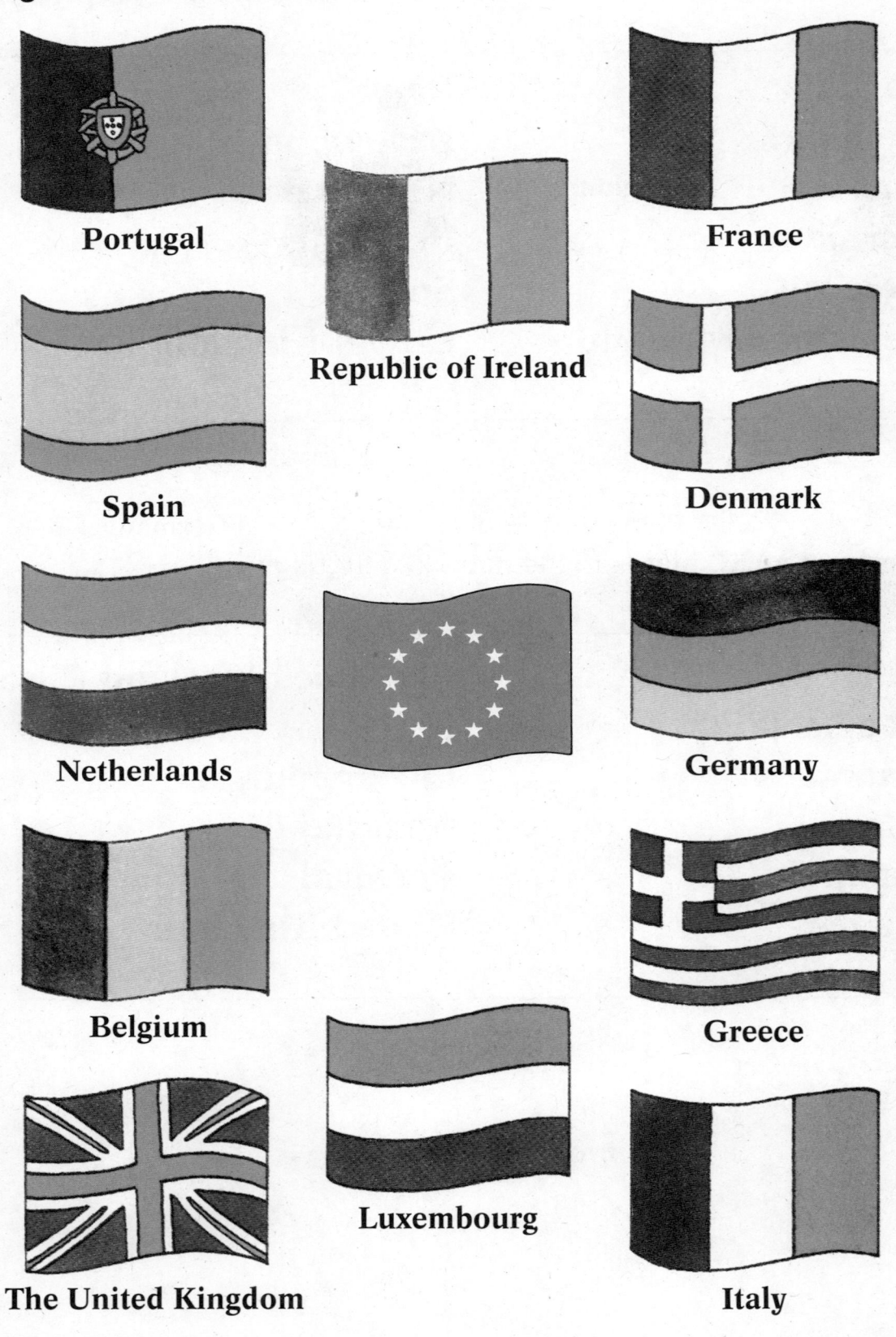

Portugal

Republic of Ireland

France

Spain

Denmark

Netherlands

Germany

Belgium

Greece

The United Kingdom

Luxembourg

Italy

Make your own EUROtic material **C**

6. The EC member states and their (car) nationality plates

Belgium
(B)

Denmark
(DK)

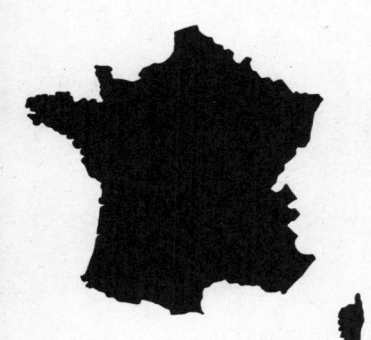

France
(F)

Germany
(D)

Greece
(GR)

Republic of Ireland
(IRE)

C *Make your own EUROtic material*

6. The EC member states and their (car) nationality plates

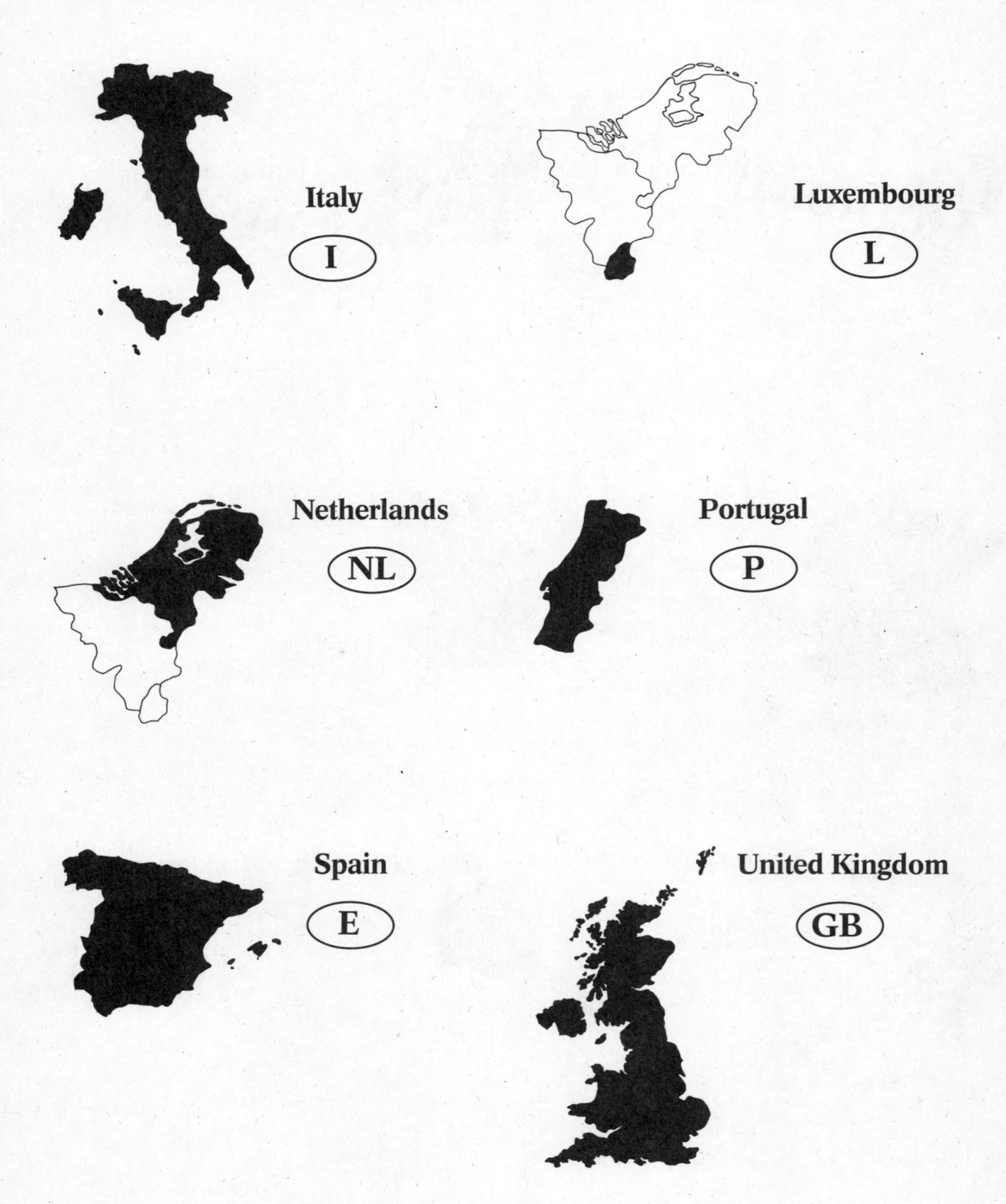

Italy
(I)

Luxembourg
(L)

Netherlands
(NL)

Portugal
(P)

Spain
(E)

United Kingdom
(GB)

Make your own EUROtic material

7. EC flag and other cut-out material

Ευρώπη

★ Europe ★

Europa

1993

C   Make your own EUROtic material

8. Map of the EC and neighbouring states

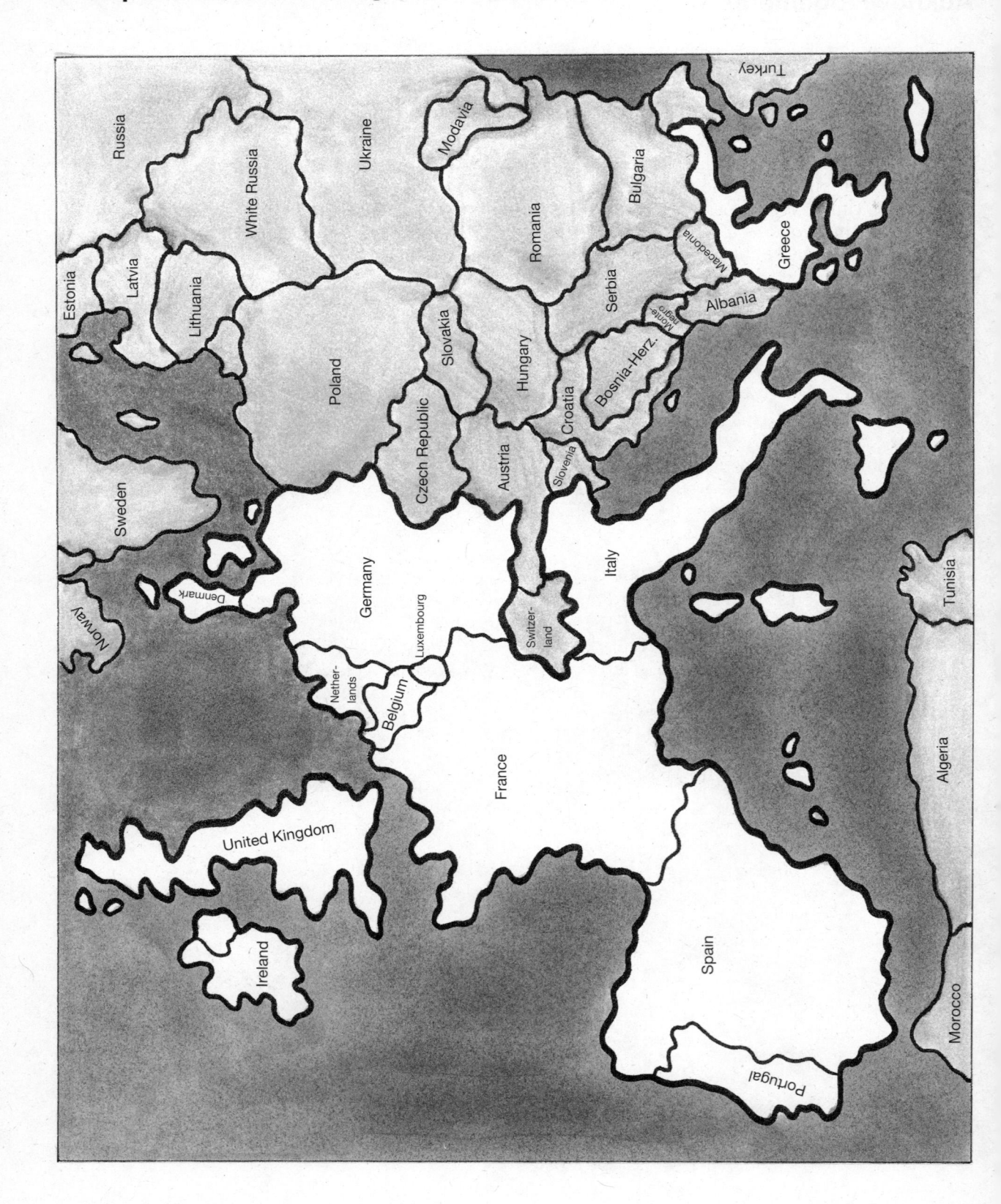

Acknowledgements

The author and publishers are grateful to the following copyright owners who have given permission for the use of copyright material identified in the text. Every effort has been made to contact copyright owners and apologies are expressed for any omissions.

About the activities
Page 9: ©Europäisches Parlament, Informationsbüro, Bonn-Center, 5300 Bonn 1.
Page 10: With kind permission of EuroPoint, Denmark.
Page 37: ©Times Newspapers Ltd., 25.05.1989.
Page 43: From *Why do we sell butter to Russia? and other common questions from the Common Market* by Nicholas Bethell, European Democratic Group.

Photocopiable material
Page 57: a),b),c),d) M. Ramos.
Page 63: 4. ©The Guardian. 6. ©Daily Mail, 31.07.1989.
Page 64: ©Daily Mail, 03.08.1989.
Page 65: a) dpa; b),c) ©Klaus Kallabis, Koppelbarg 7, 2000 Hamburg 53.
Page 66: d) dpa; e) ©Klaus Kallabis, Koppelbarg 7, 2000 Hamburg 53; f) agence photographique de presse international jean guyaux;
Page 67: a),b) ©The European, 05.11.1992.
Page 68: a) PHOSPHORE Nr. 96 BAYARD PRESSE 1989; b) Koommissionen for De europæiske FællesskaberPostbox 144, Kopenhagen; c) Textausschnitt aus PONS Reisewörterbuch Spanisch, Stuttgart 1980, abgelöst durch Neubearbeitung 3-12-518641-2, Stuttgart 1992; d) Müszaki Könyvkiadó, Budapest; e) Europese Almanak, 1990. Europese Commissie, Den Haag, Nederland; f) from *Tral'silento* by Edmont Privat. Budapest 1989; g) mit Genehmigung entnommen aus 'Langenscheidts praktisches Lehrbuch, Japanisch, Bd. 1', Langenscheidt-Verlag, Berlin und München.
Page 69: h) ©Hergé/Casterman; i) ©Sábado, 03.06.1989; j) from *Spotkania*. Ein Polnischlehrwerk für Erwachsene von Alina Köttgen. ©1989 Max Hueber Verlag, München; k) from *Yes Problem* by Latif Demirci. Dönemli Yayincilik As., Istanbul; l) Commission of the European Communities, Brüssel; m) ©La nuova provincia, 24.01.1990.
Page 70: a) Author: Hans Werner Rodrian; b) Evangelischer Pressedienst (edp); c) afp.
Page 71: d),e),f) from *Der Milliarden-Joker*, Binnenmarkt '92 aktuell by Karl von Wogau/ Klaus Löffler/ Dieter Mitzka, ©EUROPA UNION VERLAG GMBH, Bonn 1988.
Page 72: Commission of the European Communities, Brüssel.
Page 73: From *A Citizen's Europe*, published by Amt für Veröffentlichungen der Europäischen Gemeinschaft, Luxembourg.
Page 74: a) Le Quotidien de Paris, 27.10.1989; b),c),d) PHOSPHORE Nr.96, BAYARD PRESSE, 1989.
Page 76: a)-l) PHOSPHORE Nr.96, BAYARD PRESSE, 1989.
Page 77: John Carvel ©The Guardian.
Page 78: ©The Telegraph plc, 1992.
Page 79: ©The Independent, 04.04.1989; ©Daily Mail, 09.03.1989.
Page 81: ©The Guardian.
Page 82: Commission of the European Communities, London.
Page 90: Commission of the European Communities, London.
Page 91: Presse- und Informationsamt der Bundesregierung, Bonn.
Page 92: Presse- und Informationsamt der Bundesregierung, Bonn.
Page 93: Kommission der Europäischen Gemeinschaften, Vertretung der Bundesrepublik Deutschland, Bonn.